INNOCENCE SLAIN

KIT KARSON

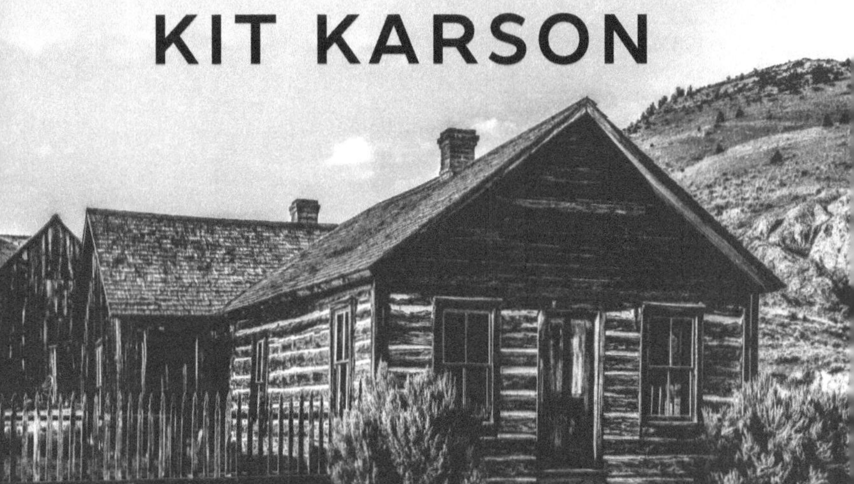

Book design by Bookery.design

ISBN 979-8-9873287-4-3 (hard cover)
ISBN 979-8-9873287-5-0 (paperback)
ISBN 979-8-9873287-6-7 (ebook)
ISBN 979-8-9873287-7-4 (audiobook)

FOR MICHELLE, CAERUS, AND JAMES,

Who add the shine

OH THAT MY HEAD WERE
WATERS, AND MY EYES A
FOUNTAIN OF TEARS, THAT I
MIGHT WEEP DAY AND NIGHT
FOR THE SLAIN OF THE
DAUGHTER OF MY PEOPLE.

Jeremiah 9:1

1

NESTLED IN THE pine forests of the Moonlight Mountains, overlooking meandering Flint Creek and the valley it waters, Anderson, Montana held itself apart from typical mining towns in that it began as an outpost for a vast ranch. The historic Anderson Ranch encompassed most of Stone County. So widespread were the holdings that hired hands on the far end of the valley were forced to spend days riding a well-worn trail to the home place for supplies and tools. Charles Anderson, family patriarch, saw the wisdom in keeping his hired men working rather than running errands. He had a blacksmith shop built on the far side of the valley to handle horseshoes, broken wagon wheels, and the like. As cowhands continued beating the trail in search of supplies, he added a dry goods store. In a wild land with provisions scarce and towns few and far between, neighboring ranches, homesteaders, and passers-through took notice of the outpost.

Ever the businessman, Charles opened his private store to the public. Soon after, he built a roadhouse and hotel, offering food, lodging, and, of course, libations. A man of morals, Charles drew the line at loose women. Saloon girls and harlots were not allowed. Unbeknownst to him, his own daughter, Clara, ran a brothel in the hotel he built for her. Charles lived out his life on the other side of the ranch, secure with the delusion that the town bearing his name was nothing less than virtuous, and no one told him any different.

While Charles found his fortune in land and cattle, others searched for treasure beneath the surface. The quest for gold and silver brought riches to a lucky few, defeat to most, and left mountains scarred inside and out. In modern times, treasure hunters come to Anderson in search of sapphires.

Formed in the depth of the earth by the melding of titanium, corundum, and iron in boiling cauldrons of magma, the beautiful gems flowed to the surface on rivers of lava. Rarer than diamonds, and some would say more desirable, sapphires are found in only a few special places. One of these is Anderson, Montana.

Modern-day Anderson offered much more than sapphires. Ski bums replaced treasure hunters in the winter months and beer enthusiasts flocked to the brewery year-round. In spite of throngs of tourists, Anderson remained a peaceful place. As head keeper of the peace, Stone County Sheriff Peter Elliot felt more than a small amount of pride for the tranquil little town.

As Peter sat, window open to the fresh summer breeze, feet on his desk, enjoying the peace, several phone lines in the sheriff's department lit up within seconds of each other.

"Boss!" Travis—the blond and buff department clerk—shouted from the front office. "We have an incident in the basement."

Peter dropped his paperback onto his desk, stood and reached for his required Stetson. "What sort of incident?"

"Something about Nancy May and a skunk."

Peter smiled. He could always count on Nancy to spice up a quiet day.

Nancy May, beloved resident of the local senior apartments and frequent source of incidents for the sheriff's department, always came out "smelling like roses" after each episode of the Nancy May show. *She may have met her match this time,* thought Peter.

"Where is everyone?" he asked.

"Tom is out at the Geary ranch checking on a trespassing complaint. Helen's on traffic duty."

"Call Helen and tell her to head this way. We might need her for… something."

Peter left his hat on his desk and instead took a hand towel out of the jail linen closet.

"Stay, Zack!" he said. The last thing he needed was a skunk-sprayed dog.

He held the towel over his mouth as he hustled his six-foot-five, 200-pound bulk down the hallway. Already the familiar, putrid scent of skunk hung in the air. He hesitated on the top step of the wide central stairway, swallowed a gag, and two-stepped his way into the cloud. Workers, coughing and gagging, pushed past him, rushing to the door and fresh air. A breeze blew up the stairway as he descended, carrying a faint scent of vomit underlying the musk of skunk. By the time Peter got to the basement, the hallways were bare, and the offices empty of people. Every door and window appeared to be open in a desperate attempt to clear the stench. Seeing no immediate threat, he walked to the end of the hallway and out the back door into a scene of chaos. People were gagging, puking, crying, and moaning in individual torment across the courthouse lawn.

He said in his loudest voice of authority, "Can anyone tell me what's going on here?"

Nobody stepped up to answer. Helen arrived in her patrol car, astonishment on her face as she surveyed the pandemonium. She rolled down her window.

"Is it safe to get out?" she called to Peter.

He nodded and motioned for her to join him.

"What happened?"

"Something to do with Nancy May and a skunk."

"Oh boy."

"That's the story, but I don't see Nancy May or a skunk," said Peter as he searched the grounds.

EMS parked behind Helen and began unloading gear.

"What do you do for skunk spray?" asked Helen.

"Not a clue," replied Peter. "Maybe EMS carries emergency spray canisters of tomato juice."

Helen snorted as the EMTs unloaded canisters of… something.

Peter laughed until he had tears streaming down his face.

"Do you need an eye rinse, Sheriff?" asked an EMT, mistaking his tears for a reaction to the skunk.

"No, thanks. I'm good," said Peter, wiping away the tears.

Rick Jones, Stone County animal control super-intendent, had his office in the basement of the courthouse. Peter watched as Rick made his way across the lawn. Obviously disgruntled, he rubbed his eyes and coughed into a towel.

"Glad we could amuse you, Sheriff."

Oh, boy, thought Peter, *I'm going to be hearing about this for the next decade.*

"What happened here, Rick?" he asked.

"Nancy May is what happened."

Helen disguised a giggle with a fake cough, earning her a dirty look from Rick.

"I don't see Nancy anywhere. Is she okay?"

"Oh, she cleared off before the skunk had a chance to spray the first time."

"Okay, Rick, start at the beginning. How and why did Nancy May happen to catch a skunk and transport it here?"

Rick sighed and blew his nose. "She walked in this morning with this black cage and started going on about catching something in her garden. I was on the phone and not paying attention. I told her to leave it by the door and I would take care of it later."

"Then what happened?"

"I got off the phone and went to have a look. I brought it into the holding cell we have for strays and opened the cage to see if it had an ID collar."

"You opened the cage without knowing what it was?" asked Helen.

Rick glared at her. "It only had a narrow opening on top. All I saw was black and a little flash of white. I thought it was a cat. It wasn't hissing or anything. Tabitha has that black and white cat, and you know how Nancy and Tabitha are always going at each other."

"So, you opened the cage?" prompted Peter.

"Yeah. I opened the cage, and the skunk ran out and sprayed me right in the face."

"Where did it go?"

"I don't know Peter. Why don't we have a skunk spray you in the face and see if you can track where it runs?"

Peter bit his lip to keep from laughing. A DMV clerk, eyes swollen and red, walked over.

"That miserable rodent ran down the hall. Every time someone opened a door to see what all the commotion was about, he let off another squirt."

"Did you see where it went? Did it make it outside?"

"Don't know. Don't care. Not going back in that building until someone says it's safe."

"Sounds like a job for animal control," said Peter. He nodded toward Rick and then turned to Helen. "I'm going to find Nancy May. She's usually in the library. Care to join me?"

"I wouldn't miss it for the world."

The Stone County library sat a block down and across the street from the courthouse. As they made their way down the sidewalk, they could see library patrons gathered on the front lawn, gawking toward the courthouse, and speculating on the brouhaha.

"What's going on, Sheriff?" called one of the spectators.

Standing front and center in the middle of the excitement was Nancy May, looking the genteel lady in her typical dainty flower-covered sun hat and matching blouse and skirt.

"Hey, Nancy May," said Peter. "Do you know anything about a skunk in the courthouse."

"Oh, yes. I dropped one off in a Skunkinator this morning. Rick said he would take care of it." She put a hand to her mouth. "Oh, no! Did it get loose?"

"Yes, it did, and the basement of the courthouse is, well, skunked."

Nancy gave him a horrified look. "Why did he take it out of the Skunkinator?"

"He thought it was a cat."

"That's silly. Why would I put a cat in a skunk cage?"

"Long story. What exactly is a Skunkinator, and how and why did you put the skunk in there?" asked Peter.

"There was a skunk in my garden every night outside the apartments. The dogs would bark at it and scare it and make it spray. You know how people let their dogs run free at night. You really should do something about that, Peter."

"I know, Nancy. Unfortunately, animal control doesn't have a night shift."

The crowd muttered and complained about the loose dog issue.

"So, what is a Skunkinator?" asked Peter.

"I found it at the hardware store. You put cat food in the box in front. The skunk waddles in to eat and the door closes so he can't get out. There isn't room for him to lift his tail and spray." She leaned toward Peter and whispered, "He couldn't resist. I sprung for the premium cat food."

"Chicken and gravy?"

"No, even better. Seafood pâté."

"I'm sure the skunk appreciated the special thought."

"Could you tell Rick I need my Skunkinator back? That one might have a wife come looking for him since he didn't make it home last night. Tell Rick if I catch another one, not to let it out in the courthouse."

"Sure, Nancy," chuckled Peter. "If Rick doesn't get that back to you right away, you let me know."

"I surely will."

"Where do we go from here?" asked Helen.

"Lunch at Dixie's Diner?"

"Not issuing any tickets?"

"I can't see where anybody did anything wrong."

"Lunch it is then."

Helen and Peter avoided the courthouse and walked to Dixie's.

2

T OURISTS PACKED THE streets these days and shops, including the brewery, catered to them. But the beer still tasted the same, so the old man came and sat and drank and watched. He didn't need a fancy degree from a university to read their mood. Nearly all the outsiders could be sifted into two categories, happy or miserable. Folks in the brewery, surrounded by friends and beer and—most nights—good music, tended toward the happy side. The old man looked outward. Bored teenagers, resigned husbands, hands shoved in pockets, shoulders slumped. *Why are you here?* Wives and mothers collecting quality time bragging points. At least the little ones were happy, giant ice cream cones and hours of digging through pails of dirt for sapphires. *What kid wouldn't go for that?*

The old man watched the couple, first on his side of the street and then the other. Just kids themselves, early twenties. Her long blonde hair, worn lose, curled down her back. She was slim, but curvy. The girl he remembered from long ago.

Ruggedly handsome described her beau, well built, and beachy blond. They would be mistaken for siblings but for the touching. To the casual eye, they were a well-matched pair, not so much on closer look. Her hair was loose, but cut well, salon colored and styled. Her clothes, tailored. Both toe and fingernails salon fresh. The old man had an eye for these things. The boyfriend wore last year's hiking boots and a faded T-shirt. His nylon shorts had seen more than one season fishing or hiking or rock climbing. She hung on his arm, laughing and talking and stopping every few feet to gaze into a shop window. He looked like he wanted to slit his wrists. *How long will this last?* thought the old man.

Not long, for as he watched, the girl turned to enter a gift shop. The boy shook his head. The girl insisted and pulled on his arm.

The boy stopped short, wrenched his arm from hers and yelled, "Enough!"

The rest was lost in cross-traffic and passers-by, but when the street traffic cleared the old man saw the boy stalk down the street and climb into a battered Jeep Wrangler. The boy sat, uncertain, eyes on the girl as she stood on the sidewalk, wearing the astonished look of a spoiled child, spanked, but stubbornly refusing to leave her spot on the sidewalk. Eventually, the boy started the Jeep, backed out of his parking space, and made his way toward the highway and home. The girl stuck her bottom lip out in a pout, shrugged, and scanned the sidewalk up and down. Her eyes passed the brewery and then quickly turned back. She smiled, waited for traffic to pass, and stepped off the curb.

Like a moth to the flame, thought the old man and he sipped his beer and made the decision. *Not my usual place for capturing moths, but I've been waiting a long time for this one.* And he waited.

3

BEING A POPULAR tourist destination didn't necessarily guarantee an abundance of enthusiastic local employees. This held true for the Anderson sheriff's department. Helen Ferguson, the only full-time deputy, covered night shift call. Barely halfway through July, endless calls dealing with summertime revelers already had her worn out. The stress of the job and issues in her personal life contributed to her burgeoning waistline and growing apathy toward a beauty regime. A long gray braid required no maintenance.

After being pummeled by fugitives and accidentally pepper sprayed by Helen in a recent apprehension, part-time deputy Tom Edwards was less inclined to sign on for shifts that could possibly involve more than routine traffic stops.

Angus McLeod, oft borrowed deputy from nearby Deer Lodge County, was well aware of need for full-time deputy help in Anderson when he walked into the Deer Lodge County courthouse.

Although he never bothered to look up the history, Angus would've bet the court houses in Rumsey and Anderson were designed by the same architect. The layout of his Uncle Jake's office, minus the notched out back corner hiding Peter's secret stairway exit, were exactly the same. Any similarity ended there. Peter's office, with a well-worn, but comfortable leather sofa along the far wall and vintage western art covering faded paint, was cozy. Angus felt at ease there, even if he was sitting in front of the sheriff's desk getting his butt chewed for some dumb thing he'd done. Uncle Jake's office, not so much. The furniture was top-of-the-line executive suite collection and, truth be told, more pleasing to look at than it was to sit on. Jake, ever worried about blemishes whether on his walls or his reputation, ordered the room painted a snowy white every other year. Instead of Western art, pictures of Jake covered the walls. Jake with the governor. Jake with celebrities. Jake with the president on a Montana fishing trip. Jake. Jake. Jake.

"It's an election year, Angus. I can't give you that promotion. What would my constituents say?"

"You're not 'giving' me the promotion, I earned it, and you can tell your 'constituents' I earned it."

"That's not how they will see it. I'm running against a tough opponent. He'll use anything he can to smear my good name."

Angus stared at the glossy white walls and the endless framed handshakes. What was that his grandma used to say? "Fight the battles you can win, Angus, and walk away from the rest." Angus, red-haired, slight and wiry, was full of energy, all focused on his job. He'd trained every deputy in the department, and he was still treated like low man on the totem pole. Seniority didn't count if you were the sheriff's nephew. His eyes wandered to a pad of notepaper laying on Jake's desk.

"Can I borrow a pen?"

"Sure, Angus. Whatever you need," said Jake, lifting a rosewood pen out of a matching holder and handing it across the desk. "The governor gave me that for helping him on his last campaign," he bragged.

Angus wrote two words on a piece of notepaper, signed his name, and handed it to Jake.

"What's this?"

"My resignation letter."

The note read, 'I quit.'

"Now, now, Angus," said Jake. "This is not a good time for you to go off half-cocked. We're short of help as it is, and I need you to train that new deputy. Hang tight until after the election and we'll look at doing something for you. Maybe a new patrol car."

You said that before the last election, thought Angus, *and I'm still waiting.*

He stood, unpinned the badge on his chest and laid it on Jake's desk.

"Take a couple days off and think about it," urged Jake.

Angus pulled his duty gun out of its holster, emptied the chamber and magazine, and laid them next to his badge. He reached into his pocket for his patrol keys and laid them next to his gun.

"Tell you what," said Jake. "You have some comp time coming. I'll sign off on a whole week. Go fishing. Fly to Mexico. Have some fun. Your gear will be here when you get back."

Angus held out his hand. "I won't be back, Jake. Good luck on your election."

With no return hand offered, he turned and walked out of the office before the other man could say another word. *After treating me as a burden for all those years, he sure is eager to keep me around,* thought Angus.

He waved goodbye to the office clerk and walked one final time through the hallway, across the wide lobby, and down the elegant split stairway leading to the main floor. He used to feel honored to work in such a grand building. Now he knew it was all superficial and replaceable with a more desirable fraternal twin in Anderson.

＊

PETER NEEDED HELP. He was more than a little excited when a filled employment application popped in his email box.

Birdie Bradshaw, age twenty-six, associate degree in criminology, Dawson Community College. No experience in law enforcement.

Peter sighed. Not ideal, but she had the basics and he had plenty of county funds to send her to the Law Enforcement Academy in Helena. He picked up his desk phone receiver and punched in the number for Ryan Beck, head of the Criminal Justice Department at Dawson.

"Hello. This is Ryan."

"Hey, buddy. Peter Elliott over in Anderson."

"Peter! Great to hear your voice. I've been expecting your call."

"Birdie Bradshaw?"

"Yep."

"What can you tell me about her?"

"Good student. Not straight As but tried hard. Dedicated."

"Character?"

"Excellent. She's a Miles City girl. Rumor is she was a partier in her younger days, but I didn't see any sign of it while she was here."

"Any idea why she went into law enforcement?"

Most people go into law enforcement to help others, sometimes because they were victims themselves. Sometimes it's a family tradition. A rare few see law enforcement as an excuse to bully others. It mattered.

"Not sure, Peter. There's something there, like she's haunted. She doesn't talk about it. But she's got a good heart and a desire to serve."

"Why does she want to come to Anderson? There are plenty of jobs closer to home."

"She said she has memories over there. Give her a chance, Peter. She has a year to prove herself or fail. A stint in Helena will clinch the deal."

"I think I will. Thanks, Ryan."

"Hey, keep me posted."

Peter pushed the button to end the call and punched in Birdie's number, surprised when she picked up on an unknown.

"Hello, Miss Bradshaw. This is Peter Elliott, sheriff of Stone County. I received your application."

Breathless with excitement Birdie gushed, "I'm so happy you called Mr. Elliott… Sheriff, I mean. It's my dream to work for your department."

"Do I know you?" asked Peter, confused at her enthusiasm.

"No, not really. You probably don't remember me. I haven't been there for years."

"Um, okay. You know the opening is for a night shift officer?"

"Yes. I'm willing to fill any open position."

"And we would send you to the Law Enforcement Academy as soon as possible. We wouldn't expect an officer with no experience to cover night shift by himself… or herself, as the case may be."

"That's fine. I'm looking forward to the academy."

"How soon can you get here for an interview?"

"Tomorrow?"

"What is it, about a seven- or eight-hour drive from Miles City?"

"Closer to six. I can leave here in the morning and be there early afternoon."

"Okay. Let's say four p.m. tomorrow. See you then."

Peter ended the call and pondered.

"Hey, Travis."

"Yeah, Boss?"

"Would you see what info you can find on a Birdie Bradshaw."

"Like a background check?"

"No. We can't legally do that until we offer her a job."

Travis came to the doorway of Peter's office and leaned against the frame.

"We have an applicant?"

"Birdie Bradshaw," said Peter. He printed out a copy of the application and handed it to Travis. "Recent graduate of the criminal justice program at Dawson. Has her heart set on working for Stone County."

Travis studied the application.

"No experience. Did she say why she wants to work here?"

"She said she has 'memories.' No specifics, but she acted like I might know her from several years ago. If the department had contact with her, would it show up on a computer search?"

"Depends on how long ago it was. Unless she was the perp, probably not."

"Knock, knock," said a familiar voice.

Travis turned to find Angus standing behind him. "Hey, Angus. How's it going?"

"Come on in, Angus," said Peter.

Travis followed Angus into the room, and they sunk into the comfortable worn leather chairs in front Peter's desk.

"Why does it smell like a den of skunks in here?" asked Angus.

Travis laughed and told him about Nancy May and the Skunkinator.

"Never a dull moment in Anderson," mused Angus.

"We have our moments," replied Peter. "Good to see you. They've been keeping you busy in Rumsey. We haven't seen you since those murders last month."

"Yeah, wasn't that some crazy stuff. I noticed the bakery is still shut down."

"Margaret bought it, you know, the cranky lady who owns the quilt shop next door."

"I thought that was a butcher shop."

"The Prime Cut," laughed Travis. "No. A quilt shop and she hated the Dahls who owned the bakery."

"Is she going to start it up again?"

"No, she sold the equipment and is having the building professionally cleaned and sanitized. Rumor is she's going to use it for quilting retreats. So, what brings you to town?" asked Peter.

"Well," said Angus, "I'm wondering if you would consider bringing me on full time."

"Wow! That would be great," said Travis. He looked at Peter. "Um, I mean, if it's okay with you, Boss."

"How does your Uncle Jake feel about that, Angus?" asked Peter, hesitant to step on the toes of a fellow sheriff.

"Doesn't matter. I resigned this morning."

"No kidding," said Travis.

"I was going nowhere there." He paused for a moment. "You know how Uncle Jake is."

"Yeah, we know." Peter reached into his desk drawer for a paper application. He handed it to Angus. "Sit there and fill this out. We'll make it official today. Another applicant is coming for an interview tomorrow and I don't want there to ever be a question about your seniority."

"So, I have the job?"

"You're already in our system so no problem converting your status to full time." Peter stood and stuck out his hand. "Welcome to the department."

4

BURNING TOAST WOKE Stacey. Smoke made her cough. A pounding headache kept her eyes closed while she processed. *Hangover? Burning toast? What?* She turned from her side and felt a sagging mattress under her back and rough blankets against her arm. Only one arm. The other was stuck in the bed. *Stuck? What?* Nothing was familiar. Stacey forced her eyes open against bright sunlight. *Everything a blur.* She blinked several times to force moisture onto her corneas. Cornea. She knew that from the biology class she taught last week in school. Her eyes cleared and her mind blurred. Nothing was familiar.

"About time you woke up, sleepy head," said a sweet-faced old man.

An old man. He looked familiar. Did she know him? Where was she? Stacey tried to speak through a dry throat. It came out a rasping groan.

The old man brought her a cup and lifted it to her lips. "You won't get your coffee in bed every day. After today I'll expect you to do the brewing."

The coffee wasn't horrible. She told her brain to hold the cup in both hands and only one obeyed. A glance at the other flipped her stomach. Her wrist was bound to the bed with a thin blue rope. *Terror.* Stacey screamed. Hot coffee sloshed across the bed and spattered the old man's shirt. The kindly features transformed into a mask of rage. He slapped her across the face with the back of his hand, bouncing her head against the wall. Stacey began to cry. Never in her life had she been hit.

"Time for you to grow up and be a woman. I need a wife, not a crybaby."

The man stalked over to an old-fashioned cast iron cookstove, slipped his hand into a faded floral oven mitt, and lifted a plate out of a warming oven. When he turned, Stacey once again saw the face of a kindly old man.

"Here's a bit of breakfast for you, sweetie," he said, pulling a wooden cane chair over to the bed. He sat, scooped a forkful of scrambled eggs, blew away the steam and held it to Stacey's mouth.

She hesitated. Pounding head, confusion, terror. The stinging burn on her face reminded her not to make this man angry. Stacey opened her mouth and let the old man feed her.

"I been alone since I left my mama's house and learned a thing or two about cookin' up vittles."

Stacey nodded. The eggs were surprisingly delicious. She chewed, swallowed, and opened her mouth for more.

The old man smiled, an expression of innocent joy, and fed her another bite.

"Would you like to try a bite of bacon? I make it myself."

Stacey nodded again, unable to find her words. He fed her a bite-sized piece.

A city girl, Stacey only knew store-bought bacon, sometimes turkey bacon when her parents were on a health food kick. This was different, yet appealing, sweeter with an unusual mix of spices.

"Good," Stacey croaked.

"You must be dry as burnt toast," said the old man. He winked. "Like those charred bits that didn't make it to breakfast."

He set the plate next to Stacey on the bed and walked across the room to a large old whiskey barrel with a spigot on the side. A row of speckled blue enameled cups hung on nails on the wall above the barrel.

Reaching for a cup, the man glanced over his shoulder and smiled that charming smile. "I have sweet mountain spring water piped directly into this barrel." He brought the cup to Stacey and held it to her mouth so she could drink. "So much better than that chlorinated tap water in some towns."

Hunger and thirst abated, she desperately needed to pee. Stacey studied the room and the man and contemplated her situation. As far as she could tell, there was only one door and that led outside. *No bathroom? Would asking trigger another episode of rage?* Stacey held her head as far as possible away from the wall.

"Um, sir?"

"Name's Ben, sweetie."

"Ben... um... uh... do you have a restroom?"

Momentary confusion passed over his face, and then realization.

"Privy's out back." He waved his hand toward the back of the cabin.

Captor and captive studied each other. Stacey looked at her bound wrist. Bewilderment followed by embarrassment clouded Ben's features. He sat on the cane chair by her side, embarrassment replaced by fear.

Ben leaned close and whispered, "I can take you ta' the privy, but you can't try an' run away. He'll hurt us."

Stacey scanned the room. "Who?"

"Ebenezer. He'll hurt us. He likes ta' hurt folks."

The urgency in her bladder overrode thoughts of escape or fear of the mysterious Ebenezer. Stacey nodded in agreement and watched while Ben expertly untied the knots binding her wrist. He helped her sit upright and sat patiently while her dizziness subsided. He helped her to her feet. Because of the headache and fogginess in her brain, Stacey suspected she'd been drugged.

Ben stopped at the door, pulled a key out of his pocket, and unlocked a padlock fastened around the door latch.

He looked at Stacey and whispered, "If we make him angry, he'll take the key."

Where is Ebenezer? Is he the one who kidnapped me? thought Stacey. Scenes of her day in Anderson came back, shopping and the fight with Kevin. After that it was a blank.

The privy was a lonely shack at the end of a long narrow trail.

"Don't want it too close to the cabin or we get the smell when the wind shifts," said Ben in explanation.

Stacey lifted the latch and peeked inside. Her bladder at crucial capacity and threatening to release, she didn't spend much time on thought before she stepped in and latched the door on the inside. Twin windows high on opposite sides of the shack illuminated a single round hole cut into a wooden bench. *Primitive toilet seat?* A quick peek into the hole confirmed her suspicions. Thankful for an elastic waist, she pulled down her skort, sat, and felt the relief. *How many gallons can a bladder hold?*

Current needs met; Stacey continued to sit. Screens covered the windows, letting in light and air and keeping out larger crawling things. Flies were not thwarted, but only one crawled along the ceiling, too many other things to draw their attention in the wilderness. She looked around for toilet paper. *Didn't they use leaves and Sears catalog pages in the old west?* Closer inspection found a coffee can on the bench. Stacey heaved a sigh of relief when she opened it and discovered a fresh roll of toilet paper inside. She cleaned herself, then stood and pulled up her skort. *Now what?* She was a city girl in the middle of the woods with some old guy named Ben who was truly afraid of someone called Ebenezer. All those years of her dad lecturing her on being safe ran through her mind. What was the name of that book, *The Gift of Fear?* The one thing she remembered him saying over and over, "Trust your instincts." She wanted to believe that Ben was a kindly old man. He reminded her of her grandpa. He fed her breakfast and brought her fresh spring water. He untied her and led her to the outhouse. He hit her. The nagging voice in the back of her mind told her he was complicit in her captivity and capable of violence. *Why am I here?*

Stacey jumped at a knocking at the outhouse door.

"Are you done in there?" asked Ben.

"Yes, sorry." She unlatched the door and stepped into fresh air and sunshine.

Ben followed her as she walked along the path to the cabin. At the door she hesitated, dreading the cabin prison and bound wrists.

"Could we stay outside for a while? I promise I won't try and escape. The sunshine makes me feel better."

"Sure, sweetie," said Ben, with a gentle pat on her shoulder. "You can help me feed the porkies."

"Porkies? Oh, you have pigs. That's how you make bacon."

"Not quite," said Ben. "Come along. You'll see."

She followed him as he turned down another path. This one led toward the outhouse, but veered off to the left, rounded a hill, and opened onto a pretty meadow filled with purple and yellow wildflowers. On the edge of the meadow sat an old, but well-kept round barn. The barn butted against a hillside and in the hill was a large door.

"Root cellar," said Ben, as he undid the catch and lifted the metal bar of the latch.

Inside was pitch black except for a sliver of light let in by the open door. The air was significantly cooler. Ben lifted a lantern off a hook in the wall and turned it on with the push of a button.

"Battery operated," he said proudly. "Not as dangerous as the old oil lanterns."

Wooden shelves lined a long narrow earthen room, each shelf filled with wooden crates. Ben lifted the handles of a wooden pushcart and wheeled it to the first shelf. Stacey walked the length of the shelves, peering into each crate. They were filled with a variety of fruits and vegetables. She recognized apples, sweet potatoes, beets, and corn.

"Do you grow these yourself?" she asked.

"Not anymore. I'm too old for that nonsense. I buy in bulk from the Hutterites."

Ben filled his cart with a mixture of fodder and called to Stacey. He turned off his lantern and hung it back on its hook. Once the root cellar door was closed and secured, Stacey followed him as he wheeled the cart toward the barn.

Doors large enough to accommodate a hay wagon were set in the front. Ben lifted a latch and opened a smaller door at the side. As with the root cellar, the barn was pitch black, but this time Ben flipped a switch inside the door and dim lights glowed overhead.

"Barely enough light to see what we're doing, but they get cranky if we wake them up during the day."

Bales of old straw lined the walls of the barn from floor to ceiling, many layers outward. Rather than being set tightly together, there were gaps between the bales.

"Burrows," said Ben. "They prefer those over stalls."

They again, thought Stacey, wondering what sort of creature this odd man kept in his barn. *At least I know they eat vegetables and not people.*

"They?" she asked.

Ben put his finger to his lips and motioned Stacey to follow him to a far corner where a short stack of straw bales filled the end of a row. He gently scraped loose straw away to reveal a sheet of plexi-glass serving as a ceiling to a burrow. Stacey leaned over to take a peek. Inside was a prickly dark gray lump. *Prickly?*

"Porcupines?" she asked

Ben grinned and nodded. "Quill pigs. Look closer. She has a baby."

Stacey could see a smaller prickly lump snuggled against its mother.

She thought of breakfast and stifled a gag. "This is what you use to make bacon?"

Ben grinned again. "Yep. I'll catch one tonight when they come out and roast it for dinner tomor-row. Better than those penned up pigs in the valley."

It's a wild pig with quills. A wild pig with quills, Stacey chanted to herself.

Ben scattered half the fruits and vegetables in his cart around the outside of the straw bales and across the floor. He then wheeled the cart outside and scattered the rest along the edge of the barn walls.

"They like to forage," he said.

"So, they're not locked in the barn?"

"No, they come and go as they please, but they always come back at dawn."

Ben pointed out several small door flaps around the lower edge of the barn walls.

"Is that why you feed them? So, they'll come back?"

"Keeps them from eating pine needles. Ruins the meat."

"Ah."

After feeding the porcupines, Stacey and Ben made their way back to Ben's cabin. One look at the desolate little house sent a shiver of dread up Stacey's spine.

"Couldn't we stay out for a while longer?" she pleaded. "It's such a nice day."

At the side of the cabin, a weathered picnic table sat decaying under an ancient apple tree. "We could sit there in the shade," she suggested.

Ben stood, wistful, eyes focused on a faraway time.

"Ben?"

A small shake of his head brought him back to the present. "Sure. My mom used to sit at that table, peeling apples. It's in bad shape, but we can give it a try."

Stacey noticed an overgrown road circling around Ben's house and up into the mountain in the opposite direction of the barn.

"Where does that go?"

Clouds dimmed the sun, blocking any warmth and much of the light. A shadow passed over Ben's face. Fear and then anger.

"None of your business! Get inside!" he growled as he shoved her toward the cabin.

Going through the door, Stacey tripped on the threshold and fell to the floor, catching herself with her right hand. She felt something give in her wrist and heard a crack. Instant pain. Ben kicked her, the toe of his boot connecting with multiple ribs. She screamed.

"Stupid, clumsy woman. Shut up and get back on that bed!"

Ben grabbed her by the hair and drug her across the rough-hewn floor.

"I said git yer worthless butt back in that bed!" He banged her head against the bed frame as he attempted to lift her onto the mattress by her hair.

Stacey whimpered in pain and fear. "Please," she whispered. "Please. Stop."

Ben muttered in disgust, dropped her on the floor, and stomped his way to the door. Stacey heard it open, slam closed, and then the sound of a key turning in a lock. She didn't care. She only wanted the pain to stop.

5

EARLY THE NEXT morning, Peter, Zack at his side, walked the few blocks from his homey bungalow on the east edge of town to the grand granite courthouse holding vigil atop Anderson's steep Main Street. The lane from Peter's house, like most Anderson roadways, was unimproved dirt. It could be called the original dirt from the original town, but every heavy rain washed several layers of that soil to the bottom of the mountain, leaving deep gullies in the roads. Anderson's current road crew of one would fire up the skid steer, load its bucket from the ever-present mound at the bottom of the mountain, and fill and pack as many road gullies as possible before the next rain.

Main Street was one of the few paved streets in town. The town council reluctantly agreed to the upgrade in order to accommodate the massive flow of tourists flocking to Anderson to hunt sapphires, eat homemade fudge, and drink craft beer.

As Peter entered the courthouse on his way to the second floor and his office, a lingering reminder of skunk hung in the air and followed him up the stairway.

Helen and Travis were at their desks filling out reports and getting ready for morning update.

"No donuts this morning?" asked Peter.

"Right here," said Helen, grabbing a bakery box off the back worktable and tossing it onto Travis's desk. "The grocery store is getting so good at donuts; I hardly miss the bakery."

Zack, trained German Shepherd and the department's unofficial mascot, stretched, yawned, and walked over to the desk for his daily donut ration.

I thought someone in the family would take over the bakery after Bob went to prison," said Travis, tossing chunks of donut for Zack to catch in his mouth.

"Nah. They all have lives of their own. They don't want to be saddled with the bakery. They probably needed to sell it to pay off debt anyway," said Helen.

"Anything exciting going on?" asked Peter. "Did you get any calls last night, Helen?"

"No, thank goodness. No drunks. No wrecks on the highway. No domestics. Everyone home in bed where they belong."

"The bottom two floors of the courthouse are on call for emergencies only because of the skunk incident," said Travis. "A clean-up crew from Missoula is supposed to be here later this afternoon."

"The mayor didn't think the smell was bad enough to shut down the sheriff's department," observed Peter. "Although, I noticed his office is closed today."

"Typical," said Travis.

"I have an interview this afternoon for the night deputy position."

"Really?" asked Helen, grinning. "I might get off Vampire Patrol?"

"Birdie Bradshaw, fresh out of community college. She sounds promising, but no experience. She'll have to attend police academy in Helena first and then train alongside you until she's ready to be on her own."

"That's okay. At least there's a light at the end of the tunnel. When's she supposed to be here?"

"Four."

"I hope the smell doesn't dampen her enthusiasm," said Travis.

"Naw. We got this. Did you find her in any records?"

"Nothing yet, but I'll keep looking."

"Why are we looking for a record on her?" asked Helen.

"She said she'd been around this area years ago. She seemed to think we might remember her."

"Not a jailbird, I hope."

"Nothing like that. Ryan Beck at Dawson gave her a good recommendation. Any red flags should show up in the interview. At any rate, we can't afford to turn down an interested applicant. Speaking of deputies, where are Tom and Angus?"

"Angus is out on a barking dog complaint. Tom called and said he would be a little late. A freezer or something went out at the store," said Travis.

Short, stout, and balding, Tom Edwards owned the local grocery store. His wife and grown children ran it so well without him, he rarely needed to be there.

Peter sent his deputies on their way and studied the pile of paper in his 'to do' box, wondering what he could do instead.

⁕

LATER THAT AFTERNOON, Helen opened the freezer in search of a comforting pint of ice cream. Empty. She lifted the keys to her patrol car off a hook by the back door and slung her purse over her shoulder. The grocery store had plenty of treats. Her second motivation had to do with the time of day. The clock ticked close to four and she wanted to check out the possible new recruit. Driving past the courthouse, Helen noticed a commotion as a cleaning crew from Missoula unpacked their vans.

She sat in her patrol car and watched as a young woman chatted with a white suited worker and then made her way into the courthouse. Definitely attractive. Ebony hair in a short pixie cut, but with the bone structure to pull it off. Slim. *Birdie Bradshaw. Who else would willingly go into that mess?* Helen sighed, pulled down the visor mirror and studied her reflection. *Time for a change.*

BIRDIE REMEMBERED THE courthouse in Anderson as a dignified granite edifice. What she found on arrival was a granite edifice, but dignity was in short supply. An assortment of disaster restoration vehicles filled the street, forcing her to park several blocks away. Workers in white jump suits, goggles, and masks scattered across the lawn with a variety of gear. The sheriff hadn't called to reschedule her interview, but other than the restoration group, it didn't look like anyone else was in the courthouse.

"Excuse me," she said, approaching a white suit.

He pulled down his mask, a full smile for the pretty woman. "Yes, ma'am?"

"I have an appointment with the sheriff. Is it safe to go into the building?"

"Safe, but not pleasant. You might want to plug your nose."

"What happened?"

"Skunk attack. I've seen the sheriff's deputies coming and going all day, but the rest of the building is evacuated. You'll find the sheriff on the second floor."

She thanked him and made her way up the sidewalk.

Skunk attack? thought Birdie. *Weird.* She peeked through the window glass of the door, peering into corners. No skunks. Thankful for a last-minute whim to dress up her outfit, Birdie pulled the colorful scarf from around her neck, held it in front of her nose, and opened the door. *Gag. Definitely skunk. Were they rabid? Was there more than one? How did they get in?* She hurried up the wide central stairway, relieved to find the stench fading the further she climbed. A placard on the second-floor landing pointed the way to the sheriff's office.

Angus sat at the shared deputy's desk in the sheriff's department pretending to type up a report. He saw the young woman enter and a pair of emerald green eyes scan the room. As they settled on him, his stomach did a flip.

Sitting at his desk tracing over a work schedule that had already been filled in, Travis glanced up and, with the eye of a body builder, accessed the perfect womanly form walk into the room. Slim, but curved in all the right places. His mind went blank.

Birdie assessed the blank stare and open mouth of the young man at the desk. It wasn't her first rodeo. She cleared her throat to get his attention.

"Excuse me. Birdie Bradshaw. I have an appointment to see the sheriff."

"Uh… um… yeah. I'll let him know you're here."

Travis hit Peter's intercom button. "She's here."

Peter noted the flush in Travis's face as he opened the office door for an extremely attractive young woman. *Oh boy.*

"Have a seat, Miss Bradshaw," he said, motioning to the comfortable leather chair in front of his desk.

Travis continued to stand at the door, a dopey look on his face.

"Thank you, Travis."

The flush turned into a blush. Travis said, "Sure, Boss," and closed the door as he left.

Older and wiser, Peter wasn't as susceptible to Birdie's beauty as the younger deputies. Despite her inexperience, she was bright, level-headed, and well educated in law enforcement. There were no obvious red flags in the interview process, but Peter worried about Birdie's looks being a distraction in the field.

As the interview reached the end, Peter asked the question sitting at the back of his mind. "Why do you want to work in Anderson?"

"Uh," said Birdie, not yet ready to give up her secrets. "I used to come here when I was younger. I have memories."

Interesting, thought Peter. *Just memories. Not good memories.*

He held out his hand. "Thank you for coming in, Miss Bradshaw. I'll review your application and be in touch. Can I recommend a place to stay tonight or are you driving back to Miles City?"

"I'd like to stay a few days and have a look around. I did see a strip motel on the way into town."

"The Sapphire Inn. Old and a bit rundown, but clean and the price is reasonable. Your other option is the historic Clara Hotel. Pricier and usually booked up months before the summer season."

"I'll check out The Sapphire Inn. Thanks."

As Peter followed Birdie into the outer office, an agitated young man burst through the door.

"I need you to find my girlfriend," he wailed.

Birdie forgotten, Travis helped the man to a chair, Peter poured him a glass of water, and Angus prepared to take his statement.

"First, your name and the name of your girlfriend," said Angus.

"My name is Kevin Pederson. My girlfriend is Stacey Nichols."

"Start at the beginning. Why do you feel we need to find your girlfriend?"

"We've only been dating a few weeks. She begged me to come here. I thought we'd be digging for sapphires or hiking to the ghost towns, but all she wanted to do was shop. She spent an hour in the jewelry store, hinting all along that I should buy her something. Really? On the third date?" He glanced at the others as they nodded in agreement.

"Go on," said Angus.

"Then she dragged me into a clothing store. I had to sit there on a hard chair while she tried on everything in the store. If I didn't ooh and aah and tell her how great she looked, she'd get mad. I finally bought her a dress just to get out of there." Kevin took a drink and sighed. "It didn't even look that good on her."

Peter glanced at his watch. He was hungry and at this rate dinner was going to be late.

"So, what happened to her?" he asked.

"I thought we'd be done after that. We could go get lunch or something, but she grabbed my arm and started pulling me into some sort of gift shop. I pulled back and told her no and she flipped out. I mean, complete psycho stuff. Yelling and hitting me with her shopping bag. I got mad and told her I was leaving, and she could either come with me or find her own way home. She stood there looking at me like I was a monster. I got in my Jeep and headed for Missoula."

"That was this morning?" asked Angus.

"No, yesterday. I fumed all the way home. Later, when I cooled down, I felt guilty about leaving her." He looked up at the others again. "She wouldn't get in the Jeep. What could I do?"

"But you came back," said Angus.

"Yeah. She had money. I figured she'd get a room for the night, and we'd work it out today. But last night her mom called looking for her. They had some sort of family gathering she wouldn't have missed. She wasn't answering their calls either. Then her roommate called this morning looking for her. No one's heard from her. I drove over hoping I could find her."

"If you write down her phone number," said Travis, handing Kevin a pad and pen, "I can put a trace on it."

"Where did you look?" asked Angus as Kevin wrote the number and handed the pad back to Travis.

"The motel, the bed and breakfast, all the bars and restaurants. I even checked at that stupid gift shop to see if she went in after I left. Nobody's seen her."

"Angus," said Peter, "call Tom and see if he's available to help you canvass the neighborhood."

"Sure, Boss."

"Kevin, we'll need names and phone numbers for Stacey's friends and family."

Travis handed the pen and pad back to Kevin.

While the crew organized, Birdie slipped out. *Not again,* she thought. *Not again.*

6

NOBODY HAD EVER called Mary pretty, not even as a child. As she grew, and the soft features of her baby face shaped and hardened into their permanent form, her rating on the attractiveness scale plummeted. A hawklike nose, dark beady close-set eyes, and the lack of an obvious chin lends a regal look to an eagle, not so much a human. Her mother told her to blame the man who fathered her, but Mary had no desire to search him out. She figured she would know him when she saw him.

By the time she was fifteen, Mary was weary of life; the endless teasing at school, the mostly drunk mother with her string of dirtbag boyfriends. At home, her sanctuary was the tiny, converted bedroom off the kitchen, most likely an afterthought addition to what had started as a sharecroppers cabin. At school, she retreated to the library. The room was usually deserted other than the occasional awkward outcast like herself. With its rows of tall bookcases and cozy reading nooks, Mary felt safe. A lifetime of taking care of herself gave Mary a resourcefulness beyond her years. Her decision made; she began forming a plan. The far back wall of the library was covered in maps, including a map of the United States. Mary studied that map. She found her hometown in the deep southeast and then traced her finger kitty-corner across the paper to the states furthest away. Her goal was to get as far away as possible. The chances of her mother looking for her was slim, but she didn't want to take that chance. Montana. Geographically opposite her home in every way.

Mary knew where her mother kept the extra cash. She waited until her mother was on a booze run and opened her closet. Mary's thin lips curled at the irony of what she saw. On the floor inside were sixteen shoe boxes, all but one contained a pair of heels. Her mother was rarely out of jeans or sweatpants, and the shoes had never been worn, but a girl could always dream. Four rows of four shoe boxes each, one row stacked atop the other. A dirtbag searching for money might check the first row or two but wouldn't likely open the third box in the third row down. The money had been safely undiscovered for decades, except by Mary.

One day, years ago, when her mother was at the bar down the street, Mary decided to play dress-up. She opened every single box and tried on every pair of glamourous shoes, until she found the box full of carefully counted and paper clipped hundred-dollar bills. Shocked at first, she studied her surroundings. If her vocabulary had allowed, she would have called it squalor. To her young mind, the box held unmined riches. She quickly replaced the money and the shoes, stacked the boxes neatly into their rows, and never a word was said. But Mary never forgot.

These many years later, box in hand, Mary hesitated. This was the day she dreamt about. Money. More than she could ever imagine and a chance to escape. What if it was no longer there?

But it was. The box was fuller than she remembered. Her plan wasn't to wipe her mother out. She had to admire her for making the effort to save all that money, but Mary also felt somewhat entitled. Hadn't she also lived in poverty all these years when relief was waiting in a shoebox in the closet? Mary took only what she needed to buy a bus ticket to Montana. She would find a job when she got there.

Wearing her best ragged dress, carrying her meager belongings and several days-worth of peanut butter sandwiches packed in a duffel, Mary walked across town to the bus station.

The man at the ticket booth eyed her suspiciously. "All alone, miss?"

Mary, aware that charm was beyond her, pasted on a smile and recited her preplanned cover story.

"Yes, sir. My dear Auntie Cora in Montana is laid up with a broken leg. Mama is sending me to help out with the youngins."

Not sure whether to believe her or not, he took her money and printed the ticket. As she reached out to take the paper, he held tight.

"You be careful out there, miss. That's a long way for a little girl to go by herself."

Mary stood as tall as her slight figure could manage. "I'm fifteen," she said.

"Yes, you are, miss," he said as he released the ticket. "Don't trust anyone and sit close to the driver."

He showed Mary where to find her bus number and departure time on the ticket and pointed her in the right direction.

Mary, no fool, took him for his word. She found her bus and boarded, even though it was ahead of schedule. She claimed the seat directly behind the bus driver and pulled a book out of her duffel to discourage conversation from other passengers. She was relieved when a nicely dressed elderly woman took the seat next to her.

I'll pretend you're my grandmother, thought Mary, and she relaxed and lost herself in the adventure of her book.

7

MISSING PERSON CASES worried Peter. Too many were dismissed as the result of over-active imaginations and too many ended in death. He needed the calming wisdom of his older brother, Paul, and the delicious home-baked cookies of his brother's wife.

The Baptist church and parsonage where Paul and Linda Elliott lived, preached, and served their flock, sat in a pretty meadow above Flint Creek on the outskirts of town. The home was built in generous proportions, with a wraparound porch and windows to match, a sanctuary in any season. During the warmer months, Paul and Linda moved folding tables onto the porch, side by side, where Paul studied and wrote his sermons and Linda, a successful author writing under a nom de plume, wrote her mystery books. Peter found them there on the afternoon Stacey Nichols was reported missing.

"Peter! So good to see you," said Linda, getting up from her chair and giving her brother-in-law a hug. "Anything exciting happening in the world of law and order that I can put in a book?"

"Could be. We had a missing person report on a young woman today."

"Is it legitimate or hysterical parents?" asked Paul.

"It sounds legit. Her boyfriend reported her missing. They were in Anderson for the day and got into a fight. He left and she stayed behind. Nobody's heard from her since yesterday afternoon, and she doesn't sound like the runaway type."

Peter sat in a wicker patio chair and gave Paul a rundown of the details while Linda went into the kitchen for snacks: tea for Peter, coffee for her and Paul, and cookies all around. "Talk loud," she said. "I can hear you from the kitchen."

Peter was grateful for Linda, not only for her cookies, but because he never had to make excuses for not drinking coffee. Coffee made him puking sick and, to him, tasted like moldy sweat socks. In a world addicted to coffee, he was an anomaly.

A steaming cup of Earl Grey tea and a plate of lemon bars appeared on the glass patio table next to Peter's chair.

"No cookies today?" asked a surprised Peter.

"We were gifted a large box of fresh lemons from a generous congregant," said Linda. "We drank lemonade until I caught Paul pouring his into the potted plant and had to think of other ways to use them."

"There's only so many glasses of lemonade one person can drink in a day," said Paul. "My stomach filed a complaint."

Peter picked up a lemon bar and bit into it as powdered sugar drifted down the front of his shirt.

"Oops. Sorry," said Linda, running to the kitchen for a hand towel. She brushed the sugar off Peter's shirt and tucked the towel into his collar as a makeshift bib. "There. You can eat lemon bars to your heart's content."

"They are good," said Peter, licking a glob of lemon curd off his lips.

Zack sat patiently at his feet waiting for crumbs.

"You don't need any more treats today, Zack," said Peter, throwing him a bite. "Go chase a squirrel."

Zack snapped up the chunk of lemon bar and happily trotted down the porch steps and into the trees beyond.

"I swear that dog understands English," said Paul.

"He knows 'treat' and 'squirrel' at least."

Peter came to visit Paul and Linda not just for cookies. Linda was not only a mystery novel writer. She also held her own as an amateur detective.

"Back to the mystery, Linda," said Peter. "What do you think happened to Stacey Nichols?"

"Well, you said she didn't seem like the runaway type. Why not?"

"According to the boyfriend, she has a strong family connection in Missoula. I called her parents and they verified that she is happy and well-adjusted. They were surprised when she didn't show up for a family gathering and genuinely concerned."

"What about the fight with the boyfriend?"

"They met at the post office in Missoula, which led to coffee at a café across the street. A few nights later he took her out to dinner. She teaches high school science and he's an engineer. That's where the similarities end. A day trip to Anderson was their third date and it wasn't going well."

"Not a strong enough connection for her to go off the deep end."

"Nope."

"If she didn't run off or do herself harm, that doesn't leave many options."

"Okay, what are they?"

"Someone could have done something to her. What else?"

"An accident."

"Ah. You're right. I'm slipping."

"That's low on the list. There's no record of her or a Jane Doe showing up at the hospital in the last twenty-four hours. It's too warm for her to have succumbed to the elements. The town is too small for her to get lost in the crowd."

"Would she have tried to hitchhike home?"

"Maybe."

"Okay. That's an option… or she could have been kidnapped."

"Without anyone noticing? Maybe. She would have to have gone willingly. Even with all the tourists in town, someone would have noticed an abduction… *especially* with all the tourists in town."

"Unless she wandered up a side street. Tourists rarely stray off the main drag."

"From the story the boyfriend told, she doesn't strike me as someone who would wander up a side street. She's a glamour girl… into shopping and spas."

"Someone could have lured her into an alley."

"True," Peter sighed. "It's sounds more and more like foul play is the most likely option." He whistled to Zack. "Thanks, guys. It always helps to talk these things out."

"Keep us posted," said Linda.

Zack jumped into his special canine seat in the back of the Explorer. Peter pulled his phone out of his utility belt and punched in the number for the sheriff's office.

"Hey, Boss," said Travis.

"Travis, were you able to get a current photo of Stacey Nichols?"

"Yeah. Her parents brought one over. They're here now and want to talk to you. Tom and Angus are showing the photo around. So far nobody remembers her except the clerks at the jewelry store and clothing store. They verified Kevin's story. The clerk at the gift shop remembers hearing a couple fighting in front of the store yesterday, but she was busy with customers and didn't get a good look at them."

"Okay. Tell the Nichols to hang tight. I'm on my way."

Peter sighed. A conversation with distraught parents was not something he relished.

The couple waiting, despite being under stress, were well groomed, the woman in a chic summer dress and the man in golf shorts and shirt. *White collar,* thought Peter. *They wouldn't throw on a pair of ragged jeans and a T-shirt because they don't have any.*

"Mr. and Mrs. Nichols?" asked Peter, walking up to the couple and holding out his hand.

"Yes," said the man, standing to greet Peter. "I'm Jarod and this is my wife, Karyn."

Karyn stood next to her husband. Dark circles under red puffy eyes belied her otherwise tidy appearance.

"Thank you for seeing us," she said.

Peter led them into his office and motioned to the chairs in front of his desk.

"Please, make yourselves comfortable. Can we bring you anything? Coffee? Tea?"

"Coffee for me, thank you," said Jarod. "I'm sure Karyn would prefer a cup of tea."

Karyn nodded in agreement.

Travis, who was standing in the doorway, turned to prepare the refreshments.

"Thank you for taking this seriously, Sheriff. We were under the impression there would be a forty-eight hour wait before you could begin a missing person search," said Jarod.

"A policy only practiced on TV and in movies. We judge each case individually. Can you tell me if your daughter has ever done anything like this before?"

"Absolutely not!" said Karyn. "We are very close. She tells us everything."

"Would she have tried to hitchhike home?"

"No! No! No! She is not that sort of girl."

Jarod slipped a comforting arm around his wife.

"Our daughter is happy and well-balanced. We are a close-knit family. What are you doing about that man she was with? Is he in jail? Have you charged him?" asked Karyn.

"As far as we can tell, he did nothing wrong. They argued and she refused to go home with him."

"Are you sure he didn't do something to her? Are you investigating him?"

"We're investigating every angle. Full cooperation from you will help."

Travis stood in the doorway, large mugs of tea and coffee on a tray.

"Travis," said Peter. "Could you show Mrs. Nichols to the visitor's lounge. She can rest there while Mr. Nichols finishes filling out paperwork."

Jarod helped his wife out of her chair and handed her over to Travis.

Travis left coffee and tea for Jarod and Peter and led Karyn into the hallway.

"No paperwork?" guessed Jarod.

"No paperwork. I needed to ask you a few questions."

"I apologize for my wife's outburst. She's been up all night worried about Stacey."

"I was told there was a family gathering?"

"Yes, an eighty-fifth birthday party for my father, Stacey's grandfather. We've been planning it for months. Relatives came from out of state. Stacey wouldn't have missed it. I was surprised she agreed to come all the way to Anderson with the new boyfriend. It's an hour drive away, but she said she needed a break from relatives."

Jarod paused and sipped his coffee. Peter kept silent. He sensed Jarod had more to say and was collecting his thoughts.

"We spoiled Stacey in many ways. I knew when I met that new kid, Kevin, it wouldn't last. He's the type that wants to go white-water rafting and mountain climbing. 'Roughing it' for Stacey is having a chipped nail and the salon is closed."

"What do you think Stacey would do in the situation yesterday? In a strange town without a ride home."

"She would have called me to come and pick her up."

"No doubt?"

"No doubt. And if she couldn't get me, she would have called her mother or a friend."

"There were no calls to either of you?"

"None. She came by in the morning and introduced us to Kevin. That's the last time we saw or heard from her."

"And everything seemed fine then?"

"Yes. Kevin struck me as a decent kid. No red flags."

"There's always the chance this was a targeted abduction. What do you do for a living, Mr. Nichols?"

Jarod looked up in surprise. "You mean like a ransom thing? I hadn't thought about that. I'm a law professor at the university. My wife works at the university library. We're comfortable, but not wealthy enough for someone to kidnap Stacey expecting a hefty ransom payout."

"You don't have legal clients who would target your daughter?"

"No. I'm strictly a professor."

"Did Stacey ever mention having a stalker or enemies who would do her harm?"

"Never."

"Okay. I assure you we are doing everything we can to find your daughter. If you think of anything else that might help, no matter how trivial, please let us know."

Jarod opened his mouth, closed it, and took another sip of coffee.

"Was there something else?" asked Peter.

"I tried, Sheriff. I tried to teach her to protect herself. She refused to learn how to use a firearm. She refused to carry pepper spray. She refused to take self-defense classes. I would read to her from *The Gift of Fear.*" He looked up at Peter. "It's a book about trusting intuition to stay safe."

"I've read it. Good advice."

"I would read that to her at the breakfast table, always hoping a little would sink in."

"This isn't your fault, Mr. Nichols. Ultimately, we make our own choices."

"Be honest with me, Sheriff. What are the chances of you finding Stacey alive?"

Peter hesitated. "Every hour that goes by lowers those chances. She's been missing over twenty-four hours and we haven't heard anything. Not good. I'm sorry."

As Peter stood and held out his hand to Mr. Nichols, Zack placed a large paw on Peter's leg and whined. *Always one step ahead of me,* thought Peter.

"Mr. Nichols, would you happen to have a piece of clothing belonging to your daughter. Something she's worn recently?"

"Uh, I'm not sure. I could look in the car. Why?"

Zack walked around to the front of Peter's desk, sat on his haunches, and gazed at Jarod Nichols.

"Oh, is your dog trained in tracking?"

"Trailing, actually," said Peter. "Tracking works on the theory that dogs follow only the scent left by footprints. Their noses are forced toward the ground to keep them on the scent. Trailing allows the dogs to keep their noses up and follow scents in the air."

"And that's better?"

"Yes, footprint scent trails can disappear on certain surfaces and are burnt off quickly on hot asphalt and concrete. Scents in the air are more stable. There may still be a scent trail beyond the gift shop where Stacey was last seen."

"I swear he knows what we're saying," said Jarod, studying Zack.

"He's been through a few missing person investigations."

"I'll look in the car. Stacey was with us on an outing earlier in the week. She may have left something."

Several minutes later, Jarod came panting through the door after a run up two flights of stairs. In his hand was a colorful scarf.

"Success! Karyn said Stacey was wearing this and then decided it was too hot for a scarf and took it off. It's been in the back seat of the car since then. This is her favorite scarf, so she wears it often. Will the scent be fresh enough?"

Peter took the scarf from Jarod and held it under Zack's nose. Zack's ears stood up straight, he whined, and headed for the door.

"It's still good," said Peter, lifting Zack's trailing harness from a peg on the wall.

8

FIFTY YEARS PAST its prime and merely utilitarian in the better days, The Sapphire Inn hadn't won travel magazine awards for quite some time, if ever. But it was clean and offered life's basic necessities if you weren't interested in modern conveniences such as air conditioning or a working door lock. The clientele of The Sapphire Inn leaned toward vacationing families on the more desirable end of things and partiers on the other. Neither group was inclined to rob its neighbors, but Birdie chose to leave her overnight bag in her car regardless. *No reason to tempt fate*, she thought, and wished every young person lived with that wisdom.

After checking in, Birdie hung her crossbody purse, 9mm Springfield pistol safely tucked inside, over her shoulders. She slipped her left hand into her pants pocket, reassuring herself a fresh canister of pepper spray was at the ready. Friends told her she was paranoid. Maybe so, but Birdie Bradshaw wasn't going to disappear and leave her loved ones traumatized. She walked the six or so blocks up the hill to Anderson's main touristy area, barely remembering that same walk three years past. Barely, because she and her friends started drinking early on in the day and were drinking as they walked, especially Selina.

Selina was the outsider in the group. She worked in the mall with Birdie, a clothing store where Birdie found a job to pay rent on the low-end studio apartment she escaped to after failing out of the university. Who knew they would have an issue with not going to classes or doing homework? She paid her fees after all, and college wasn't cheap. Birdie continued to lie to her parents about classes and grades and all-night study sessions, regularly checking the university semester schedules in case her parents checked up on her.

"That sounds like fun," said Selina when Birdie relayed her weekend plans of a trip to Anderson, a group of friends, and a concert in the park. *Good music and lots of booze.*

"I could drive," offered Selina, fingering her ever-present bead and crystal hippy necklace. "You know. Be the designated driver."

Why not, thought Birdie. Selina, long dyed black hair entwined with beads, gauzy ankle-length skirt, and Birkenstocks was too gypsy queen for Birdie's tastes, but, hey, she'd be too drunk to notice.

"Sure," said Birdie. "We'll leave after work on Friday. You'll have to pay your share of the room and gas."

When they got to Anderson and The Sapphire Inn, Selina pulled several bottles of cheap wine out of her canvas duffle.

"I thought you were going to be designated driver," said an annoyed Birdie.

"Don't worry. I'll be sober in time to drive us home," replied Selina between chugs of wine.

Birdie was too drunk to care. The group walked the six or so blocks to the touristy area of Anderson and somehow managed to find their way to the park. That was the last time Birdie saw Selina.

The next morning, a pounding on the motel room door competed with the pounding in Birdie's head.

"You girls have half an hour to pack up and be out or you'll be charged for another night. We have to get your room cleaned for the people coming in," yelled an irritated voice on the other side of the door.

Birdie groaned, rolled over, and blinked her eyes clear to look at the bedside clock. Almost noon. The air reeked of booze and vomit. A lump in the bed next to her turned its head her way. She was relieved to see it was her friend Amy and not a strange man she'd picked up in a drunken blackout, although it wouldn't have been the first time. Lumps in the other bed and one in the corner of the room stirred and groaned and cursed the day. Birdie made her way to the bathroom, contemplated the vomit covered toilet seat, decided she couldn't wait to pee, and hovered as best she could.

Very little conversation took place as the room full of hungover girls took turns stumbling to the bathroom to relieve themselves. They silently gathered their things. All had passed out in the clothes they wore the day before and didn't feel the need to change for the ride home. Duffels were tossed in the back of Selina's Jeep Cherokee. Each girl crawled into her seat. A bottle of Tylenol made the rounds. Not until they were settled, seats leaned back, and eyes closed for the drive home, did they realize the vehicle wasn't moving. Birdie, in the front passenger seat, opened her left eye enough to get a good look at Selina in the driver's seat. Selina wasn't there. The seat was empty.

"Where the heck is Selina?" she groaned.

A series of grunts and "I dunnos" emanated from the back seat. Birdie cursed, opened her car door and rolled out, barely catching herself from falling to the ground. She brought her left palm to her pounding temple and her right to her rolling gut and proceeded to vomit on her shoes. *Definitely Selina's fault,* she thought, as she shuffled back into the motel room.

The housekeeper was already in the room, nose and mouth covered with a bandanna in a futile attempt to filter out the stench.

"You girls should be ashamed of yourselves."

"Yeah, whatever. Is Selina in here?"

The housekeeper looked around the room, hands held out, palms up.

"Do you see anyone else in here?"

Birdie shook her head. Pain.

"Does that duffel bag belong to your missing friend?" asked the housekeeper pointing at a canvas duffel in a corner.

"Yeah, that's hers." *Where could she be?*

Birdie walked around the housekeeper, stooped to zip the duffel closed and hooked the handles over her arm.

"You didn't see anyone when you came in?"

"Nope."

Birdie walked out of the room and around the back of the Cherokee. She studied the parking lot and the other rooms in the strip motel. *Where could she be?* After throwing the duffel into the cargo area, Birdie let herself back into the vehicle.

"Did any of you see Selina this morning?"

"No. Maybe she went home with a guy," said Amy. "Who cares. She can find her own way home."

"This is her car, genius," snapped Birdie. "That would be grand theft auto, and besides, we don't have the keys."

Multiple groans from the other passengers.

Birdie wiggled her cell phone out of the back pocket of her too-tight blue jeans, searched her contacts, and hit the call button for Selina. It went straight to voicemail. *Why did she have her phone shut off?*

"Hey, Selina. We're all sitting here in the parking lot waiting to go home," she said, after the beep. "Please give me a call as soon as you get this message."

The girls waited for half an hour, got too warm sitting in the Jeep, and walked six blocks to a Dixie's Diner for breakfast.

"What are we gonna' do?" whined Amy.

"Does anyone know someone who will come and pick us up?" asked Birdie.

"My sister will come," said Rachel. "She'll be annoyed, but she'll come. We'll have to pay for her gas."

"Call her already," muttered Stephanie.

Two hours later, the girls piled into a faded-red compact sedan, not caring that they were cramped.

Out of spite for her desertion, they left Selina's vehicle unlocked in the motel parking lot. Weeks later, the motel had it towed, anything of value already cleaned out by opportunistic thieves.

Monday morning, Birdie walked into the clothing store, a practiced speech at the ready, detailing Selina's offenses. But Selina was not there. Birdie poked her head into the manager's office.

"Is Selina sick today?"

"No call, no show," sighed the manager. He was used to employees quitting without notice. *Young people these days. No sense of responsibility.*

Birdie felt a twinge of unease. Selina was weird, but she was reliable. Her till was always counted out to the penny. Her sales area was organized. Birdie felt in her heart that something horrible had happened to Selina in Anderson, and Birdie and her friends had deserted *her*, not the other way around.

Birdie took the next day off, claiming a family emergency. Selina may not be family, but as far as Birdie was concerned, her disappearance was an emergency. She drove to Anderson and to the courthouse and found the sheriff's office on the second floor. The courthouse, a large brick and granite edifice built in the late 1800s, was designed to take full advantage of natural light sources. Large windows dominated most areas; the sheriff's office was no exception. Birdie found it surprisingly bright and cheerful. Several desks were scattered around the room, with a paper-strewn worktable along the windows at the far end.

"Can I help you?" asked a deputy sitting at the desk closest to the entrance.

Three years later, Birdie would still remember that man. Peter Elliot was etched on the name plate on his desk. She would remember the pity in his eyes as he explained to her that young adults came to party in Anderson on a regular basis and, not infrequently, an acquaintance would report one missing. Usually, the missing party would show up after they sobered up, and rarely did anyone bother to notify the sheriff's department. Without some sort of evidence of foul play, an adult wasn't considered missing.

"But she left her car sitting in the motel parking lot. She was supposed to drive us home," pleaded Birdie.

"Happens all the time," explained Peter. "We'll keep her information on file in case anything turns up."

But nothing did. What Birdie didn't know was Selina had left her family in Chicago on bad terms many years previously. They didn't know she was missing and didn't care.

Angry and feeling misunderstood, Selina had hopped a Greyhound bus and rode it as far as Montana. Montana, the land of endless sky and wilderness. Who would look for her in Montana? With money she had stolen from a previous employer, who wouldn't turn her in because she caught him cooking the books, she paid cash for her Jeep at a discount car dealership in Billings. From Billings, Selina drove further west. Further into the wilderness in her mind. She landed in Missoula and the job at the clothing store and felt safe. No family to harass her. No ex-employer to track her down. Other than rent, no debts owed to anyone, moral or otherwise. Nobody besides Birdie to report her as missing and nobody was listening to Birdie.

For Birdie it was a life changer. She couldn't change the booze-filled weekend that led to Selina's disappearance, but she could change her ability to make a difference. She quit the boozing. She fessed up to her parents about school and they invited her home to pull her life together. She took a year to pay off ill-used student loans, applied to community college, and registered for the criminal justice program. If the sheriff deputy in Anderson wouldn't look for Selina, she would become a deputy and look herself.

9

WHILE WORKING IN Rumsey, Angus lived at home with his parents. He saved his housing budget for an apartment above the Moonlight Mountain Brewery in Anderson. Truth be told, for the past several years, he'd spent more time on duty in Anderson than Rumsey. His favorite spot for off-duty relaxation was the back corner table inside the brewery. An ideal spot for several reasons, partly because it was a great place to overhear local chatter and had led him to breaking his biggest case—a poisoning by pie—and also because it was the favorite off-duty relaxation spot of Holly Noelle, owner of The Sapphire Pit tourist attraction and keeper of Angus's heart.

"Hey, Angus," said Holly, holding a pint of golden beer in one hand and a basket of hot wings in the other. "Split a basket of wings?"

"Been saving your seat."

She pulled out the nearest stool and set the wings between them.

"What's new? Are you here working a case for Peter?"

"As of today, I'm officially a full-time Stone County deputy."

"Really? That's great. I'll bet Peter's happy."

"I guess."

"I hear Peter interviewed a new deputy today."

"Yeah. Birdie Bradshaw."

"I hear she's a looker."

Angus blushed. "Ah, she's okay. You know how it is, a new girl in town and everybody's lookin'." He pinched a wing out of the basket, ripped off a hunk of meat with his teeth, and chewed.

Holly sipped her Summer Sunshine, a favorite local brew, the familiar citrus scent washing the dust of the day from her nose. What she really wanted to know was how Peter reacted to the new girl, who was described to her as "drop-dead gorgeous."

"How are you guys going to handle things out in the field with a pretty young girl to watch out for?"

"We manage fine with Helen."

Holly laughed. "Not the same thing. Helen's like a mama grizzly bear. She'll take care of all of you."

"True." Angus didn't want to talk about other women. He wanted to talk about Holly, and he and Holly together. "Hey, are you going to the concert Saturday?"

"The one in the park? Are the bands any good this year?"

The rest of the world was blocked out as they discussed bands, packing the cooler, and strategic seating for the best sound experience.

Across the street, Peter stood in front of the gift shop, Zack at his side. Officially off duty, he was dressed in olive-green nylon shorts and a faded gray Eddie Bauer T-shirt, too grungy to look like a tourist, but not likely to be mistaken for a sheriff investigating a disappearance. Following in the footsteps of Kevin and Stacey was predictable up to the gift shop. Kevin had parked at the bottom of the hill. Stacey drug him past the ice cream shop and into the jewelry store. An hour there. Kevin was a patient man. Peter had wanted to run out after the first minute. A bench sat inside the door next to a table laden with coffee urns and plates of goodies, specifically placed by the management to appease the menfolk. Happy men stayed longer, and their wives spent more money. Next was the clothing store where Kevin, patience tank running on empty, had bought the dress. Next was the gift shop where Peter now stood. Every detail of Kevin's story was double checked and verified. Stacey wanted to keep shopping. Kevin was out of patience. There had been an argument. Stacey refused to leave. Kevin stormed back to his Jeep and left town without her.

Peter tried to put himself into Stacey's head. What was she thinking, or better yet, what was she feeling? He had to think like a pampered young woman. She would be angry with Kevin. Scared? No. She had plenty of money and a cell phone and doting parents ready to drop everything and drive over from Missoula to pick her up. A ride home wasn't on her radar at this point.

Peter's growling stomach jolted him out of his thoughts. Mixed aromas of spicy pulled pork, hamburgers, and hot oil wafted across the street from the brewery food truck. It was lunchtime when Kevin and Stacey fought. It was dinnertime now, but the food truck would have been open and cooking then, too. Stacey would have smelled the delicious food as she stood and watched Kevin drive away. The brewery. Peter looked around. No one was paying attention to the grungy guy with his dog. He pulled Stacey's balled up scarf out of the ziplock bag in his pocket and held it under Zack's nose. Zack sniffed the air, wandered back to the gift shop doorway, sniffed the air again, and then pointed his nose toward the brewery. Peter crossed the street, letting Zack lead him, as they followed the ghost of Stacey's footprints. Zack trotted over to the order window of the food truck.

"Are you following scent or are you hungry?" Peter asked Zack as he reached down to scratch his ears.

She would have gone to the food truck and ordered first, thought Peter. That made sense. *Would she have gone inside the brewery?* He studied the crowd filling the sidewalk tables around and in front. Yuppies from Missoula. These were her kind of people and it had been a beautiful day. She would have stayed outside. Peter ordered a pulled pork sandwich and homemade chips at the food truck, with a hamburger and fries for Zack. He was officially off duty, so asked for a house special dark ale at the brewery window. It wasn't Cold Smoke, but it would do. After collecting their food, Peter once again let Zack have his lead. He sniffed the air and followed his nose to the furthest table on the far corner of the sidewalk next to the alley. Not the most popular location, the table was still empty in this early dinner hour. Zack sniffed around the table, focusing on the chair closest to the sidewalk, back to the road. Not Peter's choice of seats, but from what Jarod had said, Stacey wouldn't be worried about situational awareness and safety. Zack pulled at his lead. He wanted to follow the scent into the alley.

"Hold on, Zack. We'll eat first."

Peter set the plates of food on the table and sat, back to the wall. He broke the hamburger into quarters and fed the first one to Zack before he took a bite of his own sandwich.

Showing up after hours and out of uniform was a carefully planned strategy. Peter had a niggling suspicion there was a local element to Stacey's disappearance. Working undercover was practically impossible when you were a sheriff in a small town but blending into a crowd of tourists was easy. He finished his sandwich and ordered another ale to nurse while he watched people. Angus and Holly came out of the brewery arm-in-arm, tipsy, laughing. They made a distinctive couple with Angus's bright red hair and Holly's ringing laughter. *Were they a couple?* They walked past his table on their way upstairs and didn't notice Peter or Zack. His experiment in blending was working. Interesting how Holly had dumped Peter in a rage because he chose to leave college for a career with the sheriff's department, yet she didn't seem to have a problem with Angus as a deputy.

"Peter!" said a voice that immediately made Peter cringe. Mavis Vallee, perfectly coifed owner and editor of the local paper, *The Anderson Chronicle*, a weekly rag that tended more toward gossip than actual news.

"Hi, Mavis."

"Peter! What brings our illustrious sheriff out to the brewery on a beautiful summer day?" She looked back and forth dramatically. "Are you undercover?" she whispered.

"Just having some pulled pork and a beer, Mavis. Nothing to hide here."

"Well, you sit right there, and I'll get you another beer. What's yer' poison? Har har."

"Actually, on my way home, Mavis, but you're welcome to my table."

"Oh, Peter, darling, I so wanted to chat with you about every little thing."

"Come to my office tomorrow, and we can chat then."

"Humph," Mavis pouted. "Oh, all right, then, but I'll hold you to it." She searched the tables for another victim, only seeing crowds of tourists, and sashayed down the street.

Peter waited until Mavis was out of sight, and, more importantly, he was out of her sight. He pulled the scarf from his pocket and let Zack have a good sniff. Zack headed directly toward the alley. An historic house and barn filled the corner lot opposite the backdoor of the brewery. Both structures were long past habitability, roofs caved in, and windows broken out, but room had been cleared on the side for several parking spaces. Zack circled through the makeshift lot, came back to a space between two cars, and sat looking at Peter.

"Is this the end, Zack? Did she get in a car here?"

Peter studied the cars. His best guess was they belonged to the bartenders on duty at the brewery.

"I can't take you inside, Zack."

Peter walked Zack to the specially designed, police dog kennel-equipped Ford Explorer and loaded him, leaving plenty of windows down for air circulation.

"I won't be long," said Peter.

He walked back to the brewery and into the bar. Bud Henderson, ever-present owner/operator and chief brew master of the Moonlight Mountain Brewery, greeted Peter with unusual enthusiasm.

"Peter! So good to see you! What brings you into my humble establishment?"

"Uh, I wanted to ask you about the parking out back."

"In the alley? Is there a problem? I don't know who owns that lot, but nobody's ever complained."

"No complaints, Bud. Who parks there besides your staff?"

"Some locals. They get tired of fighting the tourists for parking spaces in front."

"Anyone in particular?"

"I don't pay that much attention, Peter."

Bud lived in the second apartment above the brewery and had a garage opening into the alley.

Then came the answer to his delight in seeing Peter.

"Are you going upstairs for pizza and beer with Holly and Angus?" he asked.

"Wasn't on the schedule. Why?"

"They have an order ready, and I'm swamped. Would you mind bringing it up?"

Peter didn't relish an awkward moment between him, his ex-girlfriend, and his new deputy, but he wasn't going to tell Bud that.

"Sure, Bud. I can do that for you."

"Great!" Bud slid a freshly filled growler across the counter. "The pizza is at the food truck ready to go."

Peter hefted the growler with a grunt and strode out the door, contemplating the impending meeting and whether he would stay for pizza if invited.

Pizza and growler in hand, he stood at Angus's door. His immediate concern was how to knock on the door with hands full of pizza and beer. He was saved from his dilemma when the door opened, and Angus stood looking at him in astonishment.

"Uh, hi Peter."

"Bud asked me to bring your dinner up."

Angus reached out to take the pizza. "We, uh, I mean me and Holly, we were about to eat. Do you want to have pizza with us?"

"No, thanks, Angus. I'm on my way to the cabin. There are some things I need to check on. Thanks anyway."

Holly came to the door and peered over Angus's shoulder.

"Oh, hi, Peter," she giggled.

Peter knew that giggle. It was the *I've already had too much to drink, and the party just started* giggle, and, for some reason, it made him angry. He shoved the growler into Angus's reaching hand, turned on his heel, and stalked down the hallway to the stairs, Holly's giggle echoing behind him.

Peter slammed the door too hard when he got into his Explorer. *Pull yourself together,* he thought. *You didn't expect Holly to stay single forever, did you?* He drove home, packed his hiking bag, and pointed himself toward the mountain. Zack always needed the exercise and the best way for Peter to clear his mind was a hike into his cabin and a night of peace.

10

"This is a good place to get off for lunch and a bathroom break."

The voice startled Mary out of her worries. In reply, her stomach grumbled. Her bladder, full to bursting, screamed for relief and her backside ached from sitting for hours on the hard seat of the bus.

"There's a nice diner next to the bus station," said the grandmotherly woman seated next to her. "It would be safer for you if we pretend we are together."

"Um, okay," replied Mary. "I need to use the bathroom, but I have a peanut butter sandwich in my bag for lunch."

"Nonsense. You'll need more than peanut butter to get you to Montana."

Startled, Mary wasn't sure how to reply.

"I was standing behind you when you purchased your ticket," explained the woman. "My name is Elaine. I'm on my way to Nebraska to visit my grandchildren."

"I didn't bring extra money for food." Mary felt the woman eyeing her ragged clothes and battered duffel.

"Lunch is on me. And when I get off in Nebraska, we'll find a suitable seatmate to take my place."

Unused to the kindness of strangers, or anyone else for that matter, Mary muttered a shy "thank you," and followed the woman down the steps of the bus. She hadn't anticipated long conversations with fellow travelers and the story of her family in Montana was weak, so she peppered a skeptical Elaine with questions about her grandchildren. Elaine, on her part, pegged Mary for the runaway she was, but felt helpless for a solution. While Mary was in the restroom, Elaine alerted the bus driver of her suspicions and he promised to watch out for Mary as long as she was on his bus. As the miles passed, and buses and drivers changed, would-be exploiters were rebuffed and the seat next to Mary was always taken by a suitable guardian.

That is until the bus pulled into Anderson, Montana. Mary's ticket was for Missoula, but the current driver worried her. His questions were too personal and his interest too keen. She watched an intense conversation between the driver and the man at the ticket counter, the driver gesturing toward the bus and the other man nodding and dialing his desk phone. Mary was ratted out and she needed to bail. So, Anderson it was. Mary told the driver she needed to use the restroom. While he was busy unloading luggage from the holds underneath the bus, she ran in the other direction, out the doors of the bus station, and wandered deep into a residential neighborhood until she was certain the driver wouldn't be able to track her.

Anderson, Montana was a small town so Mary easily made her way back to the main street when she was sure the bus would have continued on its way. Unfamiliar with churches or shelters, Mary sought out what she knew, the local dive bar. And such as it was, she arrived at the Rustler's Roost.

"You're too young to have a drink, lassie," said a rugged red-headed bartender with a heavy Irish brogue.

"Only looking for a job and a place to sleep."

The clientele of the Roost were robbers and cheats, but they weren't abusers of children.

"Come on back and we'll have a talk with the boss."

And so, Mary was given a job cleaning up in exchange for a cot in the back. She was allowed to keep whatever money she found on the tables and floors after hours, which turned out to be quite a lot. Mary stayed and grew and flourished under the watchful eyes of a band of thugs.

11

E ARLY MOUNTAIN MORNINGS clutched the crispness of the night and held it captive in the shadows and shades before sunny tendrils found every last hiding place. Zack chased squirrels and Peter breathed in the morning dew, frustrations from the previous day washed away. Soul clearing was how Peter's brother would describe it, but then, Paul was the poet in the family. Peter just knew a night in the mountains made him feel better.

Anderson deputies had certain expectations of Peter. A creel of fresh trout after a night spent at his mountain cabin was high on their list. Not wanting to disappoint, Peter was at the edge of his small lake at first light, fly rod in hand, feet tangled in his line.

Peter was not a good fisherman. His secret was his mother's Magic ET dry fly. He spent many an evening bent over a vise and hook, wrapping hackle and dubbing into thread to form her creation. She called the fly ET because it resembled no earthly insect. The magic happened when it skimmed the surface of any lake or stream. Fish found it irresistible. The upper reaches of trees and bushes around the lake were decorated with abandoned ETs, the result of Peter's wayward casting. Patience and persistence rather than skill filled his creel.

That morning, as usual, persistence paid off. Limit caught, Peter carefully stowed his rod—his father's—in its case, shouldered his pack, and began his hike down the mountain.

Peter wanted to inspect the brewery's unofficial alley parking lot before the business day, and he needed to do that before his employees gathered for their morning donut and discussion ritual. He stopped at his house to shower, change, and pick up his Explorer.

The parking area was devoid of cars and the town devoid of people, so Peter unhooked Zack's leash, gave him a good sniff of Stacey's scarf, and let him snuffle unrestrained. Meanwhile, Peter crisscrossed the lot, hoping for a hint of what happened to Stacey. He followed Zack to the ruined shells of buildings, using his flashlight to inspect the decaying interiors.

Nothing suspicious caught his eye and Zack showed no interest in the buildings until he began sniffing at a fluttering bit of white stuck in a pile of rotting timbers. He sat, turned, and looked at Peter. Peter donned a pair of exam gloves and plucked the paper from the wood. It was a business card, sturdy paper, rectangular, and blank on first inspection. He turned the card over and read, *Flint Creek Valley Bed and Breakfast, Anderson, Montana*. That was it, no proprietor's name, no specific address. Peter sorted through his brain but knew of no Flint Creek Valley Bed and Breakfast in Anderson or otherwise. Zack circled around to the same spot as the night before, sat on his haunches, and looked at Peter.

"Ok, Buddy. We can assume Stacey, willingly or otherwise, got into a vehicle parked in roughly that spot. Judging by your reaction, she touched this card at some point."

Peter whistled to Zack and loaded him into his kennel seat. He then opened the glove box, took out a fresh evidence bag, and dropped in the card.

❖

A BAKERY BOX sat on Travis's desk. Angus, Tom, and Birdie Bradshaw gathered close.

"That doesn't look like it came from the grocery store," said Peter, as he walked in the door, Zack at his heels.

"It's from a bakery in Missoula. A thank-you for the interview yesterday before I head home," said Birdie.

A gourmet selection of baked goods filled the box. *No dieting today*, thought Peter, picking out a maple long john.

"Where's Helen?"

"She had a domestic call last night that kept her up for a while, so she went home to bed," said Travis, not mentioning the look of panic on Helen's face when she saw the bakery box.

Peter set the creel of fish on Travis's desk.

Travis opened the lid and peeked inside. "Fresh out of the lake?"

"Pulled them out this morning."

"Wish you would tell us your secret," said Tom.

"Just tons of hungry fish in that little lake," said Peter. He handed Travis the evidence bag. "This may be a lead on that missing person case. Have you ever heard of a Flint Creek Valley Bed and Breakfast?"

Travis studied the card. "There are a few bed and breakfasts in the county, but I've never heard of this one. It doesn't have a name or address."

"Yeah," said Peter. "I thought that was weird, too. See if you can track that business down, also check for fingerprints, and, if possible, where the card was printed."

Officially, Travis was the department secretary and dispatcher, but he originally began his career as a sheriff's deputy. A domestic dispute call found him trying to protect the wife in the dispute, only to find out she was the aggressor in the situation. Travis went to the hospital and the woman was charged with resisting arrest and assaulting a police officer. Travis re-evaluated his career in law enforcement to a behind-the-scenes role, but he was an excellent investigator, so all research projects fell on him.

"Where did you find this?" asked Travis.

"The lot behind the brewery. Brewery staff and some locals use it for parking."

Travis sifted through the map of streets and alleys etched in his brain.

"Aren't there a couple old buildings falling apart on that lot?"

"Yeah. Whoever owns it doesn't seem to be around or care if it's used for parking. It gives locals an option away from tourist traffic. Zack pinged that as the last spot Stacey Nichols was before he lost her trail. He also trailed to this business card stuck in a pile of wood on the lot. If we can trust his nose, and we can, she touched this card before she disappeared."

"Do we know who usually parks there?" asked Angus, interest piqued for a new investigation.

"Bud didn't have any specific names. He said locals. We also need to question any brewery employees who worked that day. Angus, why don't you take that angle."

"Sure, Boss."

Angus studied the goodie box and chose a cheese Danish, taking a bite as he walked to the door. "I'll keep you posted," he said around a mouthful.

"Birdie, come into my office and we'll talk about that deputy position," said Peter.

"Yes, sir!" She jumped up and followed at Peter's heels into the office, Zack close behind.

Instead of going to his cushion in the corner, Zack stayed next to Birdie. When she sat in the chair by Peter's desk, Zack laid his head on her lap and let her scratch his ears.

"I guess you have a yea vote from Zack," said Peter. "The next basic training class at the police academy in Helena doesn't start until early September. With no prior experience, that limits what you can do. We can rotate you through every area, but you wouldn't be on your own for a while."

"I'm ready and willing to learn."

Peter pushed a stack of paperwork in her direction. "First things first. I need you to fill out pre-employment paperwork. If you're able to stay in town for the next couple days, I want you to follow Travis around and learn the office side of things."

Birdie was disappointed and it showed. She wanted to dive headfirst into this missing person case. It was personal.

"Travis is a top-notch investigator. You'll learn excellent skills working with him," said Peter. New recruits always wanted to hit the ground running. He knew. He was once the new guy stuck in the office.

"Okay. Sure. Thanks," said Birdie, attempting enthusiasm and missing the mark.

Peter smiled and winked at Travis who was standing in the doorway listening. Birdie wouldn't be disappointed at the end of the day.

That left Peter needing an assignment for himself. He would watch the front office and answer the phone while Travis worked with Birdie. As long as things were quiet, he could do what he did best. He went to his office, sank into his chair, put his feet up on the desk, and thought. *Stacey Nichols had not been in a desperate situation. She had money and doting parents. There was no record of her calling her parents for a ride. Had she tried to call a friend? If so, a friend hadn't come forward. Would she have decided to stay in town for the night? Who gave her the card for the bed and breakfast? Did she toss it away on purpose or drop it on accident?* Peter didn't have enough information and felt frustrated and inadequate. He busied himself with routine paperwork to bide his time.

Evidence bag in hand, Travis motioned for Birdie to follow. In the back corner of the office, wedged between the long worktable and an eight-drawer antique oak file cabinet, a door led to a narrow set of stairs.

"Creepy," said Birdie under her breath.

Travis laughed. "That's what I thought the first time Peter brought me up here."

The top of the stairway opened out into a large room, bright and clean, with windows on three sides. Birdie was surprised and impressed.

"This is our investigation room. We process fingerprints, store and analyze evidence… we even have a dark room for developing film."

Travis opened a door in the back to a room filled with chemical trays, rinse tanks, and other paraphernalia of bygone days.

"Cool," said Birdie. "You actually develop film? I didn't know you could still buy film."

"We use digital most of the time, but it can be altered. When there's a chance a photo may be needed as evidence in court, we take film shots and develop them in here."

"I'd love to learn how to do this."

"Helen does most of our film developing. It's kind of her baby. We'll set you up for a day in here with her."

"That would be great."

Travis closed the door on the dark room and led Birdie to a glass-fronted cabinet sitting on a counter across the room. It was at least three feet wide and would have skimmed the ceiling in a modern building, but, typical of the late 1800s, the ornate tin ceilings in this courthouse were pushing ten feet in height.

Birdie gasped. "A CA-3000! Wow! This is a top-of-the-line fuming chamber. These are expensive. Your department must have a heck of a budget. I expected a small place like this would have to send evidence away for fingerprint processing."

"You've used one of these?"

"No. I saw one during a forensics lab tour in the city. We mainly sat through lectures in school. They taught us a few low-cost methods for processing fingerprints, assuming we would all end up in rural departments with skimpy budgets. So, did you get this with some sort of grant?"

"There's a forensic buff in town with money to burn... you know, watches all those crime scene investigation shows and donates more than we need for training and equipment. This fuming chamber just showed up one day."

"Cop wannabe?"

"No, genuinely loves the science."

A refrigerator stood at the end of the counter next to the chamber. Travis opened the door, took out a small plastic vial, and held it up for Birdie to see.

"Super glue. Cyanoacrylate."

"You keep it in the refrigerator?"

"It keeps longer that way. We also date when it was opened." He pointed at a date written in black sharpie on the side of the tube. "Super glue thickens as it gets older and can affect how well it vaporizes, which can affect print results. Normal shelf life is only about a month after it's opened so we date it and throw it out after a month."

"Do you use top-of-the-line super glue, too?"

"With super glue it's not so much the price as the consistency. Gels are high viscosity. They don't spread well. You want one that has a more liquid consistency. Clem, our benefactor, spent hours in here testing different brands and styles of super glues with various temperatures, humidity levels, and fuming times, and narrowed down the best combinations for every type of surface."

Travis opened a drawer under the cabinet and pulled out a binder. He flipped through sheet-protected pages until it opened to a chart.

"This chart will tell you the best way to program the chamber depending on what type of material you're trying to get a print from."

Birdie studied the chart and then flipped through the binder. Included were instructions on programming the fuming chamber and records of items processed along with case numbers and pictures of prints developed.

From the bottom of the stairway, they heard a click-click-thump. Pause. Click-click-thump. Pause. Birdie looked at Travis. He raised his eyebrows and walked over to look down the stairwell. Glancing back at Birdie, he grinned.

"Here's Clem now."

Travis clipped down the stairs, then came back lugging a large black plastic box.

Behind him stood a glamorous older woman, snowy white hair in loose waves adorned with a rose-pink ribbon. She wore a matching pink shirt dress and pumps.

"Clementine Cordelia Smith," said the woman, holding out a hand to Birdie. "You must be Birdie, our new recruit."

"Yes, ma'am," said Birdie, extending her own hand. "Very pleased to meet you."

"Nice strong handshake. Good. I like strong women. I spent most of my life out punching cattle with the men. When my dear Howard passed on and the children scattered, I sold up and decided to spend the rest of my days as a lady of leisure."

"Yes, ma'am." Birdie was not often intimidated, but here was a woman who could no doubt hog-tie her in eight seconds flat.

"Enough of the 'yes, ma'am.' Call me Clem."

Clem turned to Travis. "Show me what you're working on."

Travis held up the evidence bag holding the business card. "We have a missing person case… a young woman from Missoula. Zack trailed to this in the last place he detected her scent. It may be the last thing she touched before she was abducted… if she was abducted."

Clem linked her arm with Birdie's and said, "Come along, Miss Birdie, I'll show you how to fumigate for prints."

"Yes, ma… Clem."

Clem noticed Travis standing next to them, still holding the black box.

"Travis, give that box to Birdie."

He handed the box to Birdie, who gave Clem a questioning look.

"A fingerprint kit for the field. When Peter called and told me he was interviewing for the deputy position, I put that together."

"Gosh, thanks so much!" said Birdie, setting the box on the countertop and undoing the clasps.

Inside were multiple storage compartments filled with powders, brushes, backing, cards, and lifting tapes. Everything needed for fingerprinting in the field.

"This is so awesome, Clem. Thank you!"

"My pleasure, Birdie. Every new recruit gets one. After I left ranching, I spent too much time in front of the television, not sure what to do with myself. I got hooked on those crime scene investigation shows, started taking online classes, and got a degree in forensic science. I don't want or need a job at my age. Helping out here gives me a chance to use my education… and it's fun."

Travis handed the bag to Clementine, who studied the card. "I've never heard of a Flint Creek Valley Bed and Breakfast. Is it new in town?"

"None of us have heard of it. That's part of our investigation."

"I'll ask around. Do you have the fuming chamber set for printing?"

"We were getting to that. Would you care to do the honors?"

"Definitely!"

Picking up the tube of super glue that Travis had left on the counter, Clem opened the door to the fuming chamber and deposited a practiced amount onto the glue tray. Travis pulled on a pair of gloves, retrieved the business card from the evidence bag, and set it in the chamber so that both sides were open to fumes. Clem closed the chamber and pro-grammed the time, temperature, and humidity while Birdie watched closely.

"All set," said Clem. "Now bring that fingerprint-ing kit over here, Birdie, and we'll practice 'Crime Scene Investigation.' "

They pulled stools up to another counter. Clem unclasped the box and began a lesson. Reluctantly, Travis left teaching to Clem and slipped downstairs. His attraction to Birdie had gone beyond physical.

Beauty, brains, and a nice personality, he was thinking as he poked his head into Peter's office to see Peter donning and straightening his required Stetson.

"Something going on, Boss?"

"A trespassing complaint over in Pine Gulch. I'll check it out now that you're downstairs. Did I hear Clem come in?"

"Yeah, she's giving Birdie lessons in forensics. That card is in the fuming chamber. I'll start working on the location of the bed and breakfast."

"Sounds good. If anything else comes along, give Angus a call."

After Peter left, Travis rifled through his desk drawer and pulled out a tattered copy of the Stone County Business Directory. He looked at the date. Three years old, but it was a start. The directory was cross referenced by 'type of business' and 'business name.' Travis looked under 'Hotels and Motels,' 'Bed and Breakfasts,' and 'Flint Creek Valley.' Nothing. He took out the Stone County telephone directory, flipped through until he found the number for the Anderson Chamber of Commerce, and dialed.

"Hi, Mabel? This is Travis over at the sheriff's department."

"Well, hello, Travis. We haven't heard a word from the sheriff's department since nothing was done about the skunk incident. What can I do for you today?"

"Uh, yeah," said Travis, choosing to ignore the jab. "I'm looking for information on a local business. Have you ever heard of a Flint Creek Valley Bed and Breakfast?"

"Did you look in your business directory?"

"Yes, Mabel, but it's three years old. Could you look it up in your current directory?"

"Did you look online?"

"The website hasn't been updated for three years either, and nothing came up when I typed in the business name. Please, Mabel. This is important."

Mabel sighed. Travis heard her chair roll back, a grunt, then another chair roll and a thud as something heavy dropped on her desk.

"If I get a hernia from lifting this binder it's on you, Travis."

"How big could a binder of businesses in Stone County be?"

"Uh, well, it hasn't been cleaned out for a while. Probably never. I should donate it to the historical society."

Travis heard pages rustle and imagined the ancient Mabel with an old-fashioned rubber fingerguard, half-moon glasses hanging on a beaded string, slowly turning yellowed pages of an archaic tome. *Did she even have a computer?*

"Hmmmm. Nope. Ah. Interesting." Travis listened to Mabel mumble and willed himself to be patient.

"There was a Flint Creek Valley Bed and Breakfast back in the 1980s, but it didn't last long. I remember that. A couple bought that old Swanson house. Beautiful house. A shame it burned to the ground. Some kind of grease fire if I remember correctly. Of course, we were all suspicious they started it on purpose to collect the insurance, but nothing could be proved. They—"

"Mabel?" Travis interrupted.

When Mabel started remembering, it could last for hours.

"Yes, Travis?"

"Did you find anything current?"

"Current for what?"

Travis's turn to sigh. "Current Flint Creek Valley Bed and Breakfast business listings?"

"Uh, no. Nothing current. You know they didn't always call them bed and breakfasts. That's a new term that began…"

"Thanks, Mabel. Talk to you later." Travis disconnected.

Interesting, he thought. *Not a current business, but the card wasn't old.*

He swiveled in his chair and logged into his computer. Anderson didn't have a print shop, but someone in a surrounding town might recognize the card. Searching revealed print shops in Missoula, Rumsey, and Nimrod. Anyone local would likely choose those towns as they were closest. Travis typed out the list of names, addresses, and phone numbers of the shops, printed the list, and began calling.

Later that afternoon, the crew gathered in Peter's office, Clem in a consulting role.

"So, what can you tell me?" asked Peter.

Birdie, excited from her morning lessons, exclaimed, "We found prints!"

"It looks like sets from two different people," said Clem. "Three fingers on the top front and a thumb print behind are large. What we would generally see in a man. A thumb on the right bottom and a forefinger behind are smaller, more likely a woman's prints."

Peter and the deputies all went through the motions in their minds, fingers mimicking holding a card and taking a proffered card from another person.

"The man takes the card out of a pocket with three fingers and a thumb and offers the card to the woman, most likely Stacey Nichols, and she takes it with thumb and forefinger," said Angus.

Nods of agreement around the room.

"Makes sense," said Peter. "Did you run the prints?"

"No hits on IAFIS," replied Travis.

"Okay, Angus, I want you to call Stacey's parents and ask if they have anything that would have only Stacey's fingerprints, something personal. You can drive to Missoula tomorrow to collect anything they find. At least we can confirm Stacey's prints on the card."

"Sure, Boss."

"Does anyone have anything else?"

"I found several print shops in Missoula, two in Rumsey, and one in Nimrod," said Travis. "I called all of them. Most said they didn't keep a record of printed business cards but might recognize the card if we brought it in. I asked if I could send a picture. They said they had to actually inspect the paper to know if it's what they use in their shop."

"Good work, Travis. Angus, take Travis's list and the card to Missoula tomorrow. See if anyone recognizes it."

"Sure, Boss, that card could have been designed and printed using a home computer though."

"There's always a maybe, Angus, but we can't risk missing a lead. Take Birdie with you tomorrow."

Angus nodded. Birdie stifled a grin, *real police work*. Travis rarely regretted stepping back from his deputy position, he knew it wasn't for him, but he was missing a chance to spend the day with Birdie.

"Did you find out anything about locals parking behind the brewery, Angus?"

"No. I interviewed the brewery employees. They all said there weren't any locals who were there every day or even every week. Some people park in back and visit businesses besides the brewery. I parked on the side street and watched for a couple hours. It was like they said, lots of different locals coming and going. But not everyone parking in that lot were going to the brewery."

"Helen, when you're on patrol, keep an eye out for any patterns, cars that are there on a regular basis."

"Sure, Boss. Anything we need to know about that trespassing complaint in Pine Gulch?"

"Bert Smells. He doesn't take care of his own fences so when his cows get out, he blames his neighbors. This morning the Hendersons came home from an overnight visit to their daughter and found a fence across their driveway."

"Did you cite him?" asked Angus.

"He didn't actually do the fencing himself. His hired hands claim they were 'confused' about the property line."

"He pulls that every time. Did you at least make him take the fence down?"

"I stood there and watched until it was done."

"Anything else going on?" asked Peter.

"We got the memo on our annual physical fitness test. It's scheduled for week after next," said Travis.

"Great," said Peter. "We can take turns going to Helena."

Peter noticed Helen's face sag. "It's not required, Helen. If you're not up to it you can skip it this year."

"Yeah, but you can get a whole week paid vacation," said Travis. "Why would you want to skip it?"

"It's been a long week," said Helen. "I'm going home and get some shut-eye before my shift starts."

"Sure, Helen," said Peter.

Travis looked baffled. "Did I say something wrong?" he asked, after Helen left.

"Yes and no, Travis. Have you noticed Helen hasn't been herself these last couple years? She let her hair go gray and she's put on weight."

"If she's worried about getting through the fitness course, she can always walk it and still earn a couple days off."

"No, she can't. It would be humiliating for her to walk the course in front of all those young officers. And it's more than that. I'm worried about her. It was hard on her after Ray ran off with that waitress."

"That waitress was hot. I'm not sure what she saw in Ray."

"Imagine how it made Helen feel."

"Yeah," said Travis, deep in thought.

Peter whistled to Zack. "Oh, yeah, would you call Helen, and tell her to pick a day. Tom's going to come in and cover so she can drive to Helena and do her firearms qualifications."

"Sure, Boss."

12

TRAVIS SHUT DOWN his computer and transferred the phones to his mobile before he left. He had a mission, but not a plan. Helen answered the door of her cozy brick bungalow, wearing a faded pair of sweatpants and worn police academy T-shirt.

"Oh, hi, Travis. Is something going on at work? I didn't hear the phone."

"No, nothing at work. Um… if you're busy I could come back later. I, um, don't want to interrupt your day."

"No. Come in," she said, opening the door wider and leading him through the front room and into the kitchen. Do you want a cup of coffee?"

"That would be great. Thanks." He looked around the room, taking in the sunny yellow vinyl-covered chairs and lemon décor.

"Sit down, Travis. Relax. You're making me nervous. Is everything all right?"

Helen slid a large mug under the dispenser of a single brew coffee maker, lifted the lid, and dropped in a pod. She pushed a button and waited while the water heated, and a fragrant stream of fresh coffee filled the mug.

"I haven't been to the store for a while. Vanilla Latte okay?" she asked as she handed him the cup.

Travis took a sip. "It's great, Helen. Thanks."

Helen sat down opposite him. "So, what brings you here, Travis?"

"Have I ever told you about my mom?"

Helen knew Travis's mom died suddenly when he was at police academy, but none of the details. "No, I don't recall you ever mentioning her."

Travis stared into his coffee cup and swallowed hard a few times. He glanced at Helen, tears in his eyes, struggling with his emotions.

"She died when I was twenty. Six years ago."

Helen stood and searched through a cupboard to give him time to compose himself. She found a box of ginger snaps and arranged a few on a plate.

"Sorry, they're not homemade."

"That's okay." A tear rolled down his cheek. He wiped it away as he reached for a cookie. "My mom made great ginger snaps."

"You must miss her."

"Yeah."

"She sounds like a wonderful person. I'd like to hear more about her."

"She was the greatest mom, always thinking of new adventures. She was so happy and fun."

Travis sobbed and Helen got up and brought him a box of Kleenex.

"What happened to her, Travis?"

"Dad died of colon cancer. She nursed him through it. It was hard on her. Us kids were all gone to college. She got really depressed. People said she was going through 'the change' so we didn't think too much about it when she started gaining weight. That's how it is with women, right?"

"Unfortunately."

"I feel so guilty, Helen. If I'd been home with her, she might still be alive."

"Oh, Travis, you couldn't stay home with your mom forever. Kids are supposed to grow up and live their own lives."

"They found her in bed. She never woke up… a combination of sleeping pills and alcohol."

"She killed herself?"

"Nobody knows. She didn't take the whole bottle of pills. There wasn't a note. The coroner ruled it an accidental death."

"I'm so sorry, Travis. I never knew."

"Helen?"

"Yeah?"

Travis held Helen's gaze. "I don't want that to happen to you."

13

Mocking voices filled the old man's head. Elbows on the kitchen table, he squeezed his skull between his hands, willing the pressure to silence the clamor, keeping him awake, enraged. Images flashed behind his eyes. Faces from the past. A mother's expression of disdain, rather than love. A father's hands of pain, rather than comfort. Worst of all, the taunting and tormenting of the school children and teachers. In his agony, an elbow slipped, bouncing his head, nose first against the wooden plank. Pain. Blood. Sweet relief as the voices faded, replaced with reality.

And then he slept and dreamt of the good things. The school janitor who had taken pity on him, let him in after hours to shower in the locker room, gave him new clothes that fit, and washed them when they were soiled. And he slept.

⋯⋯•◆•⋯⋯

LEFT ON THE rough plank floor, Stacey slept in fits, mostly when exhaustion overtook pain. A pampered and protected life had not prepared her for her current circumstances. Her wrist, bruised and swollen, was no doubt broken, as were her ribs. Full bladder screaming for relief, Stacey contemplated her options. She had no sense of time but knew a night had passed and a new day begun. Sunlight pushed through fly-specked windowpanes, warming the air and a patch of floor in the center of the room. Stacey pulled herself carefully into the healing sunbeam, ribs protesting, gaining enough energy from its warmth to assess her situation. The most immediate need: relieving her bladder. She stretched her legs. Nothing wrong there other than stiffness from the night and she felt foolish for having slept on the floor rather than the bed. She coiled her legs and pushed herself up with her left hand, rising first to her knees and then to her feet. Some dizziness, but not enough to bring her down. She considered her surroundings. A stack of dishes, long dry, waited in a rack by the sink. Stacey recognized the glass shape of a large mason canning jar in the pile and, with halting steps, made her way across the room. Thankful once again that she was wearing an elastic waist, she pulled the skort down with her left hand and reached for the canning jar. *The wide mouth style,* she thought. *Perfect for a makeshift urinal.*

On her feet, warmed by the sun from the window, and bladder relieved, Stacey was ravenously hungry. She thought, ironically, most captives were not left with a refrigerator and cupboards full of food. No microwave and she wasn't sure she could handle the cast iron stove, but there must be something that didn't require cooking. Most of the food consisted of staples: flour, meat, eggs. There were no fresh vegetables or fruit, but there was bread and cheese and butter, and a jug of milk. Stacey managed to make a sandwich and poured a glass of the milk with her left hand. She sat in a kitchen chair to eat, amazed at how good a dry cheese sandwich could taste to a starving person. While she ate, she studied the cabin. Two windows filled the room with sunlight, one above the kitchen table and one over the sink. Both were old-fashioned twelve pane sash windows and Stacey could see the one next to her was nailed shut. Even if she broke a pane, the opening was too small to fit through. She would have to break the frames also. Remembering the scrape of a key in the lock when Ben left, she was sure the door was locked, but stood and walked over to it to check. Yep. Locked. She walked over to the sink and checked the window there. Nails were pounded in every few inches along the frame. In a spurt of optimism, she pulled up on the sash and jiggled the frame. Solid. As Stacey stepped back from the window, she heard a key in the door. Ben. Her stomach clenched in fear. Would it be the sweet old man Ben or the angry violent Ben? She didn't know if her being up walking around would pacify him or make him angry so she stood frozen in place, watching as the knob turned and the door swung open. Ben looked surprised to see her.

"Well, hello, sweetie. I didn't know you were coming to visit today."

He blinked several times. Bewilderment and then embarrassment crossed his face as he realized Stacey was his prisoner.

He cleared his throat and said gruffly, "I see you found something to eat."

"I made myself a sandwich. I hope that's okay. I was really hungry."

"Sure. Sure. Do you need to use the bathroom?"

Stacey nodded, not wanting to tell him she had already used the mason jar. A trip outside was a chance to escape.

In his confusion, Ben reached for her hands, expecting them to be tied. He noticed the swollen and bruised right wrist.

"How did that happen?"

Stacey was aware for the first time that there was something terribly wrong with Ben besides his volatility. *How could he not remember his violent attack?*

Not wanting to trigger more violence, she said, "I tripped and fell."

Ben seemed genuinely concerned. "I'll wrap it up tight. That'll do the trick."

He glanced around the sparse room, apparently looking for something useful to bandage a broken wrist.

"Tell you what. I'll run into town today and pick something up from the pharmacist."

"Maybe I could come with you? See the doctor?"

"NO!!!!"

Ben turned and let himself back out the door. Stacey heard the key in the lock and sat at the table and cried. She hurt. She needed the bathroom. She wanted to go home.

⁌●◖●◗●⁍

THE GIRL WAS hurt. What was her name? Sandy? Shirley? Something with an S. She needed a doctor but letting her go would rile Ebenezer and nothing was worth that. He needed supplies anyway, so Ben got into his old pickup truck and turned it toward Anderson.

He studied the shelves in the pharmacy. He was used to doctoring cuts and scrapes for himself and Ebenezer. He bought antibiotics now and again from the local veterinarian when the porcupines were ailing and, truth be told, used those same remedies for himself. He was at a loss how to mend the girl's hurt wrist. Not normally socially inclined, Ben studied the young lady behind the pharmacy counter. Not a friendly face, but his only option. He braced himself, and inched up to the counter, hoping for advice. The pharmacist, young and busy and full of herself, had no time for a "doddering old fool," as her mother would say. Besides, she saw the desirable Sheriff Elliott come in and, according to local chatter, he was single. She wasn't going to let him leave without noticing her.

"What?" she said rudely.

"W-w-wrist. A s-s-sore wrist. What can I do?"

Kirsten, the pharmacist, rolled her eyes. "Your wrist is sore? Do you have arthritis?"

"N-n-no. A friend fell and h-hurt her wrist. S-s-wollen." Ben internally berated himself for being so weak, but willed the anger to stay hidden.

"Maybe she should see a doctor. It could be broken."

"No! She doesn't need a doctor. It's not broken," he said, anger overtaking his shyness.

Kirsten saw the sheriff studying the paperback rack at the end of the aisle. She grabbed an Ace wrap off a shelf, tossed it in Ben's direction, and hurried toward Peter.

"Hello, Sheriff. Can I help you find anything?" she said, putting on what she thought was her most charming smile.

If rattlesnakes could smile, thought Peter. "No, but you could go back and help that old man you were being so rude to." He replaced the book he was considering, turned and walked to the checkout counter.

Realizing her mouth was hanging open, Kirsten snapped it shut and pushed past Ben, who stood frozen, terrified. His mind hadn't worked law enforcement into a trip to the pharmacy scenario. Ben didn't know how the girl had come to be in his cabin, but he knew Ebenezer was involved and sensed she was a prisoner rather than a guest.

A young mother looking for Band-Aids for a crying child jolted Ben out of his daze. By then Peter was checked out and gone. Ben studied the shelves for painkiller. *She must be in pain,* he thought. He found something that looked familiar and made his way to the cashier.

14

Life brings many crossroads. Ben was no exception. His decisions were clouded with confusion and anger from his perpetual need to appease Ebenezer. If he had a choice, and he never had a choice when Ebenezer was involved, he would spend his days tending to his porcupines. He would pick apples, and bargain with the Hutterites for vegetables, and make porcupine bacon. Sometimes life was peaceful, and Ben could forget about the bad times for a while. Then he would come home and find a girl in his cabin, always his cabin and never Ebenezer's, and he would be bewildered. *Why was she here? How did she get here?* He would hope for a while that she came to stay with him to be a companion and helpmate, but the girls were never content. They would cry or scream or turn their faces to the wall in silence. Eventually they would disappear, and life would go back to normal.

Ben parked his old pickup truck at the crossroads. The path forked in three directions, one to the right and up the hill to Ebenezer's house, the other to his doorway and the girl. *Susan? Sarah? Something with an S*, the third to the left and around the hill to the porcupine barn. After the stressful visit to the pharmacy in town, Ben didn't have the mental energy to deal with Ebenezer. He knew the girl was hurt and in pain, but he didn't have the strength to deal with that either. He opened the truck door, left his purchases in the bag on the seat, and walked slowly along the path to the porcupine barn.

Stacey heard the pickup drive to the cabin. She heard the truck door open, and slam shut. She waited for the sound of a key in the lock, never knowing if the man entering would be friendly or violent. She waited and waited and waited. He didn't come. To manage her pain, Stacey eliminated lessor discomforts as well as she could. She kept her bladder empty using the mason jar. She kept her hunger at bay with cheese sandwiches. Exhaustion allowed her to sleep. In between times, she thought. Giving up was not an option. If her life as a spoiled princess taught her one thing, it was determination. Determination guaranteed she would get what she wanted and what she wanted now was to be home. Recent days taught her she couldn't overcome her captor physically. She needed to outsmart him, or them.

Fresh air and routine chores calmed Ben's anxieties. He scattered feed for his flock and delighted in a new batch of babies. He picked a fat male to harvest. The girl would appreciate a good meal. He would tend to her wounds, give her pills to ease her pain, and cook for her. He imagined comfortable companionship as they ate and chatted into the evening.

Stacey heard the key in the lock. Her first reaction was fear, her second, courage.

Be his friend, not his captive. This is temporary. You have not been abandoned. You are going home.

The man who walked through the door was gentle Ben. His face held a giant smile, and his hand held a giant lump of bloody meat. Stacey stifled a scream.

"I butchered a big fat quill pig for supper."

"That... uh... sounds wonderful."

Ben placed the skinned and gutted porcupine in the sink and washed the blood away, all the while humming a simple tune. Stacey watched, afraid to start a conversation, never knowing what would set him off.

"Roasting would take too long," said Ben, turning and dropping the meat onto the countertop. "I'll slice this into steaks and fry them. Are you hungry?"

"Starving," lied Stacey. "That looks delicious." *Gag.*

Ben unclasped a sheath on his belt, pulled out a knife, and began slicing chunks off the porcupine. Stacey eyed the knife, pondering possibilities. She moved stiffly and painfully from the bed to a kitchen chair, putting herself closer to Ben and the knife. Her groans and shuffling drew Ben's attention.

"I'm sorry, sweetie. I forgot all about your medicine in the truck. I'll finish here and go get it."

Please leave the knife. Please leave the knife, she thought.

Ben finished slicing and laid the knife on the counter next to the meat. He stooped and opened a cupboard, noisily sorting through pans. Stacey pushed herself off the chair and walked as fast as she could toward the counter, cursing the broken ribs that slowed her. Her eyes stayed on the weapon. She was next to Ben, reaching out when he stood with a large cast iron skillet in hand. He looked surprised to see her standing next to him.

Thinking fast, she said, "Is there anything I can do to help?"

Ben shooed her away. "You're hurt, sweetie. You sit over there, and rest and I'll take care of this."

Hiding her disappointment, Stacey hobbled back to the table. She watched as Ben lit the stove with a match. He placed the skillet on a burner, scooped a large spoonful of lard out of a tub, and scraped it into the pan. When it began to sizzle, Ben forked each slice of meat and gently laid it in the pan until every piece was frying. He opened a cupboard above his head and searched through a variety of glass canning jars, finally selecting one filled with dark purplish chunks in matching liquid.

He turned to Stacey and held up the jar. "Pickled beets?" he asked.

Sure. Why not? thought Stacey as she nodded her head. *I'm not sure what a pickled beet is, but it couldn't be worse than fried porcupine.*

Ben once again rummaged through the lower cupboard and pulled out a small saucepan. He lit another match and another burner on the stove, then popped open the flat metal lid covering the canning jar and dumped the contents into the pan.

Stacey had to admit to herself that the sizzling meat smelled delicious, and her stomach growled in agreement. Ben turned the meat with a fork and stirred the beets with a large wooden spoon as wisps of steam floated overhead. While the food cooked, Ben opened another overhead cupboard and lifted down two flowered china plates and brought them over to the table, placing one in front of Stacey and the other on the other side of the table. He took two blue-tinted hobnailed drinking glasses out of an adjacent cupboard and set them next to the plates.

They look like the glasses Grandma used, thought Stacey. Between feelings of nostalgia, the warmth of the cooking stove, and sounds and scents of a home-cooked meal, Stacey began to relax.

Ben turned off the burners. He wrapped a pot-holder around the handle of the frying pan, brought it over to the table and forked several small chunks of meat onto both of the plates. He returned to the stove and did the same with the saucepan of beets. After he replaced the beet pan on the stove, he picked up his knife and washed it well in the sink and then brought it back to the table, first cutting Stacey's meat into bite-sized pieces and then his own. Stacey watched as he cleaned the knife and slid it back into the sheath on his belt. Disappointment in her missed opportunity showed on her face.

"Is this okay, sweetie?" asked Ben, mistaking her glum expression for disappointment in the food.

"Uh, yeah." She thought quickly. "I was hoping I could take some pain medication before we ate."

Ben looked at his plate. His stomach growled. "Okay, I'll go get it before the food gets cold."

He walked to the door and opened it, glancing back quickly at Stacey.

"I'm not going to take the time to lock this so don't go anywhere. Ebenezer would be angry," he warned.

At this point, Stacey didn't have the energy to try and run and it wouldn't take long for Ben to catch her. She nodded her head and waved him through the door with her good hand.

He was back in less than a minute with a white paper pharmacy bag. He sat at the table, opened the bag, pulled out a bottle of pain medicine, twisted it open and shook out a couple oval white capsules.

"Here. These should help."

Ben looked at her swollen purple wrist laying on the table. "I'll wrap that up after we eat."

The pills went down easily as did the food. The porcupine meat was fatty and tasted like a wilder version of pork. As long as she didn't dwell on where it came from, Stacey could stomach it all right. The beets were sweet and spiced with cinnamon and cloves.

"Did you make these?"

Ben, lost in his own thoughts, jumped at the sound of her voice.

"Naw. The Hutterites."

By the time Stacey finished her meal, the painkillers had kicked in. Her pain wasn't gone, but it was numbed, and she felt better than she had in days. That, a full stomach, and the warmth of the cabin made her drowsy. She struggled to stay awake, still hoping for a chance at the knife.

I'll take a short nap and when I wake up, Ben will be asleep, and I can slip the knife away.

Those were the last thoughts she had until the next morning when she awoke in bed with sun streaming through the dusty windows. The cabin was empty. Ben had gone sometime in the night, taking his knife and Stacey's hope for escape with him.

15

"WHERE ARE WE going first?" asked Birdie, buckling her seatbelt and settling in for the ride to Missoula.

Pretty Birdie was accustomed to undivided attention from men. Angus seemed nervous and distracted.

"Angus?"

He twitched and blinked a few times.

"Are you okay?"

"Uh, yeah, sorry." Angus reddened under his freckles.

Well, that's more like it, thought Birdie.

"I was thinking about something else," he said.

"Or someone else?" teased Birdie.

"Yeah. Kind of."

"Care to share?"

Angus glanced at Birdie, still embarrassed. "Last time I went to Missoula on an investigation, a crazy lady and her dog attacked me. I was out on medical leave for a couple months. It still bothers me a little."

"Yikes! What happened?"

"The dog came out of nowhere and tore into my leg. I managed to zap it with pepper spray, but by that time the crazy lady was at me with an aluminum bat. She broke my arm."

"What did you do?"

"I zapped her with pepper spray, too. The dog was put down and the lady went to jail."

Birdie tried to imagine herself in that position. Would she be able to keep her cool and handle the situation as well as Angus?

"Were you scared?"

Angus paused and thought. "It happened so fast I didn't have time to be scared. Now that it's all over, driving back to Missoula triggers the memories."

EARLY THAT MORNING, Helen stood watching the sun peek over a gap in the mountains.

When was the last time I saw a sunrise? she thought.

She turned and pulled a coffee pod out of a rack and loaded it into her coffee maker. First thing she did when that slimeball Ray ran off was dump his leaky old twelve-cup coffee maker with the chipped and stained carafe and buy herself a single serve brewer. No flavored coffee for Ray and she wasn't allowed to have any either. Besides the fact that she brought in the bulk of their income, he controlled the purse strings and declared specialty coffee a waste of 'his' money.

'His' money. Snort. *I wonder if that hussy waitress is supporting him in the manner to which he was accustomed?*

After a long luxurious shower (Ray only allowed five minutes) Helen dressed in a comfortable pair of jeans and a long-sleeved tee. No buttons to remind her of her weight. Today was the first day of her new life. A new attitude, a new look, and a new Helen. She loaded several gun cases into her Explorer. Unlike the annual physical fitness test, Helen wasn't worried about passing the mandatory annual firearms qualification. She could outshoot most of her peers in both handgun and rifle competitions. But that was tomorrow. Today, a beauty salon. A haircut and color, and high hopes for her new diet. Heck, maybe she would even splurge for a facial and pedicure. Ray wasn't worth the worry when he was around. Time to move on.

"Why are you going all the way to Helena for a haircut?" asked Tom, when she explained the need for an extra day off.

"Oh, it's not only that. I need to do some shopping," she answered.

What she didn't tell him was that she couldn't deal with the questions and the gossip and the whispers behind her back she would experience in The Emerald Salon, the only salon in Anderson.

Helen turned off Main Street and onto the highway. She took it slower than usual and enjoyed the drive. The scenic route to Helena wound through a pastoral mountain pass, often declared the most beautiful in Montana.

"I've kind of let myself go," Helen told the beautician when she was settled into the styling chair.

"Divorce?"

"Yeah. He ran off with a waitress." Helen hung her head as a surprise tear rolled down her face.

"No worries, honey. Mine did the same thing. We'll get you lookin' so hot, he'll be begging to come back."

"Oh, I don't want him back."

"Neither did I," laughed the beautician. "But tellin' him to get lost and slammin' the door in his face was the best day of my life."

Helen laughed and felt a release in her soul. Yes, today she was moving on. She didn't hesitate in opting for the entire *Queen for the Day* package. A facial, pedi, and massage followed the color, cut, and style. When she looked in the mirror, she hardly recognized herself. Her hair was now a warm brown with caramel highlights cut in a bouncy bob. Where was that sad and dowdy frump who walked in the door? All the money she was saving after Ray left gave her plenty to pay for the day plus a generous tip. Back in the Explorer, she flipped down the vanity mirror and stared and stared and laughed with joy.

"I may not be Birdie Bradshaw, but for an old lady, I still got it!"

Next was clothes. The frumpy ill-fitting generic jeans, and stained, faded T-shirts she wore on her days off were going in the trash. She was pretty sure they weren't fit for charity donations. Helen hadn't cared about clothes since before she married Ray. Spending money on clothes for her hadn't been on his necessity list either and the sheriff's office supplied her uniforms.

Opting for a chain store where she could remain anonymous, no salesclerks asking her size and clucking in disbelief, Helen purchased knit pants, comfortable, but well cut, and blouses lacking buttons to strain. The trick was to find them large enough to cover without looking like she was wearing a tent. On the verge of a meltdown, it occurred to her that she hadn't thought about food all day until that moment.

No more filling emptiness with food, she thought.

In celebration of her new life and new outlook, she took herself out to a nice dinner before driving to her hotel.

• • • • •

ANGUS AND BIRDIE drove back to Anderson with no leads on the business card printer, but in possession of a computer tablet belonging to Stacey Nichols.

"It even has the password written on a sticky note. The Nichols gave us permission to look through it for clues," said Birdie when they showed it to Peter.

"Did anyone touch it before it was sealed in that plastic bag?"

"No. Everyone is a detective with all those CSI shows on TV. The Nichols had a box of rubber gloves that Mrs. Nichols uses for housework. They said they used the rubber gloves and doubted anyone other than Stacey ever touched the tablet. Most people have their own computers and no need to borrow anyone else's."

"I wonder why Stacey had a sticky note with the password if she was the only one who used it. Most people have their passwords memorized."

"They said she changed her password every three months for security reasons, and she would complain about not remembering the new one for the first few days. She started writing it on a sticky note. We're lucky she recently changed it."

"Good work," said Peter. "Birdie, you would have the best grasp of any of us on the type of social media sites or apps Stacey would be using. After you and Travis lift prints off the tablet, work on looking through her files. See if you can come up with a reason anyone would want to hurt her."

"Do you think she was abducted by someone she knew?" asked Birdie.

"Lesson one, never assume anything. Work every possibility."

16

HELEN WAS HALFWAY through her first cup of coffee the next morning before she realized her long braid was gone and remembered her new look. She hurried to the bathroom and admired the woman in the mirror. A little tousled from the night, but wow. Just wow. Shower, wash, blow dry and ta-da! A chic bob. During her shopping trip the day before, Helen bought a tube of mascara. A little updo for her face to keep up with her hair. She dressed in a freshly pressed uniform, brushed her teeth, and took the stairs to the hotel breakfast nook. Skipping breakfast was not an option. She needed the energy for the day of shooting skills testing. She passed by the waffle maker and danish case, imagining the day when her uniform buttons would lay flat with no gap. Eggs for protein and fruit was all she needed this morning. After eating, she drove to the shooting range with more bounce in her soul than she'd had, well, since she couldn't remember when.

At the range, Helen opened the back hatch of her Explorer and unloaded the bag with shooting gear, ear and eye protection, and ammo. She grasped the case holding both rifle and pistol in her other hand and lugged them across the parking lot to the shooting range. After claiming a bench, she lined up for her turn to check in. An instructor from the police academy, Adam Henry, who she had known and admired for years, was manning the booth. He barely gave Helen a passing glance until she filled out the registration card and he read her name.

"Helen?" he said, looking up and studying her hair and face. "Wow! You look great."

"Yeah, I've been in kind of a slump. I decided it was time for a change."

He handed over her name badge and participant number, taking longer than necessary to release the papers.

"Seriously, you do look great."

In her younger years, Helen would have blushed. "Thanks, Adam."

"Maybe we could get together later?"

"Uh, sure." Helen couldn't hold back the smile. *Was she supposed to play hard to get? She'd been out of the dating game too long.*

Helen did her best to block any thoughts of Adam and new possibilities. Qualifying took concentration. She wasn't going to throw her career away on silly romantic daydreaming.

After completing the first two rounds of testing and feeling confident in her performance, Helen sat on a bench and watched her peers, mostly men, complete their rounds. She willed herself not to look in Adam's direction and, instead, lifted her face to the sun, stretched and relaxed her shooting muscles. She smiled to herself. Life was good and she was at the top of her game.

Leaning back to enjoy the warm sunshine, Helen put her hands down on the bench to brace herself and felt a lump of goo ooze between her fingers. *Yuck!* Birds are indiscriminate and the bird who chose to relieve itself on Helen's bench was no exception. She lifted her hand and grimaced. *Is there anything grosser than bird poop?* Well, probably, but nothing came to mind. She glanced around. From years gone by, she remembered an outside waterspout by the trees at the back of the shooting range.

The spout was there and functional with enough pressure to blast off even the stickiest of bird poo. Unfortunately for Helen, it was also well used.

Adding Helen's hand scrubbing to others before her created a large mud puddle and the mud was gumbo. Gumbo, being primarily clay, is slick when wet and Helen, not paying attention, stepped into the thick of the puddle on her way back to the benches. Her feet flew out from under her, accompanied by a loud ripping from the seat of her pants.

In an exercise of worst-case scenarios, this was not on the top of the list, but that didn't ease Helen's embarrassment. She scanned the area for witnesses. All clear. Everyone else was either shooting or watching the shooting. She rolled over, pushed herself upright and wished a glob of bird poo on her hand was her only problem. She was now covered head to toe in mud, including everything that seeped through the ripped seat of her pants. *So much for impressing Adam.*

Smile gone and on the verge of tears, Helen racked her brain. Who could she depend on? She needed help. Her emotional heart panged as she realized she couldn't call on her adult children. They abandoned her in favor of their father. Ray was the fun one, she was the provider. Helen pulled her cell phone from her utility belt. Travis answered on the first ring.

"Hey, Helen. What's up?"

"Uh, yeah. Hi, Travis. I'm in an awkward situation. Kind of embarrassing."

"Uh, okay. What's going on?"

Helen explained.

"Sit tight. I'll be there ASAP."

Travis went to the cupboard where extra uniforms were stored and searched through piles of pants and shirts until he found Helen's size. From another pile he grabbed an official Stone County Sheriff's Department windbreaker. He thought briefly about underwear and decided that was too personal. Helen would have to figure that one out on her own. He stuffed the clothes into a county duffel bag and poked his head into Peter's office.

"Hey, Boss. Helen needs me to bring something to her in Helena."

Peter raised his eyebrows. "What would that be?"

"A change of clothes. I'll explain later. Could I borrow your Explorer?"

Sometimes it was best to let things slide.

"Sure, Travis. Don't make me regret it."

"Thanks, Boss." Travis smiled and pumped his arm in victory as soon as he was out of sight.

Helen retreated to a back corner bench and chewed at her fingernails, resisting the urge to run to her vehicle. She checked her watch every few minutes, willing a time warp to pick Travis up and magically deposit him at the shooting range. She wasn't scheduled for another shooting session until after the lunch break, but she needed Travis to bring her fresh clothes before then. She couldn't stay sitting on the bench while everyone else left for the cafeteria.

Travis jogged through the halls of the courthouse, not allowing anyone the chance to stop him for a chat. Let them think he was rushing to a police secretarial emergency. He waited until he was out of town to turn on the emergency lights and step up his speed. He may be a clerk now, but he was still trained in high-speed pursuit.

Morning session over, the shooters wandered back to their gear bags, congratulating the top scorers and razzing others. Helen sweated and sunk low on the bench. She pulled out her cell phone and pretended to be in the midst of an important conversation, glancing around occasionally, searching for Travis.

Travis turned off the light bar several blocks before the policy academy entrance. He didn't need someone asking Peter why his clerk was rushing to shooting qualifications. With the entire state gathered for testing, someone was bound to comment.

Travis recognized Adam Henry from his time at the police Academy.

"Hi, Adam. I'm dropping off some gear for Helen."

"Sure, Travis. She looks great, doesn't she?"

"Uh, I guess," said Travis.

He walked into the observation area of the shooting range, searching for Helen's familiar gray braid.

A woman he didn't recognize turned, saw him, and frantically waved him over. Confused, he approached the woman, realizing as he got closer that the woman was Helen.

"Wow, Adam was right. You do look great, Helen. When did you do all this?"

"Yesterday," said Helen with a half-hearted grin. "I came a day early. I was feeling so good about myself, and now this."

"No worries." Travis zipped open the duffel and pulled out the windbreaker. "Wrap this around yourself."

He handed her the duffel. "Here's a fresh uniform to change into."

"Oh, Travis. You're the best!"

Helen tied the windbreaker around her waist before she stood. She gave Travis a bear hug and slung the duffel over her shoulder.

"I've got to get back. Is there anything else you need?"

"A son like you, Travis. Thank you for coming to my rescue."

The hole in his heart left by his own mother's death grew a tiny bit smaller and he smiled to himself all the way home.

"Everything okay?" asked Peter when Travis walked into the office.

"All good. You should see Helen."

"Uh, why? Is she okay?"

"She's great. You'll see."

They heard the familiar 'click, click' of woman's high heels on the back stairway and watched as Clem opened the door leading to the forensics room.

"Hey, Clem," said Peter. "I didn't hear you come in."

"You were on the phone. I didn't want to disturb you."

"What are you working on?"

"I finished those fingerprints you had going on the computer tablet and compared them to the business card in that missing person case. The prints on the computer match the smaller prints on the business card."

"No doubt?"

"No doubt."

"Thanks, Clem. That confirms Stacey Nichols touched that card."

"Did Angus and Birdie have any luck finding who printed the card?"

"Not in Missoula, at least there weren't any records. We still need to check Nimrod and Rumsey. Kind of a longshot."

They listened as at least two sets of footsteps came down the hallway. Angus and Birdie walked in the door. Travis smiled and blushed.

"What have you two been doing?" asked Peter.

"I took Birdie on a tour of the county roads so she would know where to go on calls," said Angus.

"It's a huge county," said Birdie. "We stopped at the Department of Transportation office and picked up a county map. A little 'old school,' but it gives me an eagle-eye perspective."

"Hey, if you're free after work, I can drive you around and show you some of the sites," said Travis.

Peter covered a smile, but Angus was oblivious to Travis's infatuation.

"That would be great, Travis," said Angus. "Driving the outskirts of the county puts me out of range for most calls, but she has to learn the area before we let her loose on her own."

"I'm hanging out at The Sapphire Inn until I find a place to live. Exploring is an improvement over that," said Birdie. "Maybe you could help me find a place?"

"Sure," said Travis. "We can get a list of rentals… or were you looking at buying?"

"It depends on what's available. I probably should at least find someplace to rent for short term. I can't keep living in the motel."

Another set of footsteps sounded in the hallway. Travis, still grinning in anticipation of evenings spent with Birdie, smiled until his cheeks hurt at the thought of the reaction to Helen's new look.

She walked through the door, smiled, and said, "Hey, everyone's home."

Crickets.

"Uh… uh… so how did qualifications go?" asked Peter, the first one to find his voice.

"Passed with flying colors. I got high score in all categories."

"Atta girl," said Angus. "What happened to your hair?"

Everyone laughed.

"You do look great, Helen," said Peter.

The main phone line on Travis's desk began to ring. He picked up the handset. "Stone County Sheriff's Office." He listened intently. "Yeah, she's here." Travis covered the mouthpiece with his hand. "Adam Henry on the phone for you, Helen. Do you want to take it?"

Helen blushed. "Sure." She took the handset from Travis. "Hi, Adam… sure that sounds great… see you then." Helen handed the phone back to Travis. She looked up to a room full of grins. "What?!"

"Hot date?" asked Angus.

Helen struggled to come up with an excuse for Adam to be in town. Nothing.

"Yeah, well, yeah," she said, her face bright red. "Gosh. What should I wear?"

Helen grabbed her bag and ran out the door accompanied by the claps and hoots of her co-workers.

17

A FRESH, PINE-SCENTED BREEZE wafted through Peter's office window. The morning briefing was over, and his deputies were out on their assigned tasks. Travis sat at his desk eagerly making out a schedule for training Birdie. Peter leaned back in his chair, stretched his legs out on his desk, and gave thanks for the rare moment of peace.

Outside his window, what had begun as a low babble of voices intermixed with the everyday rumble of passing cars and foot traffic, quickly escalated into angry shouts and amplified placations. Zack lifted his ears and growled.

"What the heck?" said Peter to his empty office.

He swung his feet off the desk and reluctantly left the comfort of his chair. His window overlooked the front steps of the courthouse where Mayor Kalinski and Mavis Vallee appeared to be holding a press conference. A van painted with the KRUD emblem of a Missoula television news station sat parked across the street. Set up on a portable platform at the back of the crowd, a camera man adjusted his equipment while a reporter holding a large KRUD microphone and clipboard called out questions. A growing crowd of onlookers filled the sidewalk. Members of the mob shouted occasional gibes directed toward Mavis and the mayor.

"Do you know anything about a press conference?" Peter called to Travis.

Travis came into the office and stood with Peter studying the crowd.

"Nobody said anything to me."

During a brief let up in the noise, a reporter's question drifted up through the window. "Does your office have plans in place to deal with the problem of these missing women?"

Travis and Peter looked at each other in astonishment.

"Missing women?" said Travis. "Plural?"

Frustrated, Peter slammed his required Stetson onto his head with more force than necessary. Something about a cowboy hat lent an extra air of authority to a western sheriff and this was one of those times Peter felt the need. He forced himself to breathe deep and slow in an attempt to curb his anger.

"Stay Zack!" he said.

"Why on Earth would they hold a press conference like this without involving the sheriff's office?" he blasted to no one in particular as he stormed out the door and down the hall.

But Peter knew the answer to that question. Mavis and the mayor were more concerned with being in the spotlight than with truth and justice.

As he stepped in front of the podium, Mavis and the mayor were forced to move aside. He chose to ignore their protests.

"Sheriff. Sheriff," called the reporter. "Can you tell us what you're doing about these missing women?"

"To which missing women are you referring?" asked Peter.

"We had an anonymous call telling us that several young women had disappeared from Anderson and a serial killer was suspected."

Peter glared left and then right at the mayor and Mavis.

"Serial killer? Several young women?" he growled.

Into the microphone he said, "We have one open missing person case, and yes, the subject is female.

We are working with the family of the subject, but at this time do not have definitive evidence of the circumstances of that disappearance."

"What about the serial killer and the other women?"

"Once again, we have one open missing person case. There is no evidence at this time that the subject was the victim of a serial killer."

"Do you think the skunk assault on the court-house was a diversion tactic by the kidnappers?"

Peter was momentarily speechless. "What?! No! There was a skunk issue involving one skunk. It was an animal control misunderstanding."

"But didn't that incident occur on the same day as the kidnapping?'

Out of patience, Peter bent down and unplugged the microphone, holding it tightly as he climbed the steps back into the courthouse.

"What was that all about?" asked Travis as Peter entered the sheriff's office.

"Someone called KRUD and told them a serial killer was abducting young women in Anderson."

"You're kidding!"

"Nope."

"Mavis and the mayor?"

"Probably. Unfortunately, there's nothing I can do about either one of them."

He dropped into the chair by Travis's desk and pulled the donut box over.

"Who eats only half of a chocolate cream filled?"

Travis shrugged.

"Well, it's mine now."

He took a bite and tossed what was left to Zack who gulped it down and then laid his head on Peter's lap for an ear scratch.

"I feel like we're at a dead end on this case and now the public is in an uproar thanks to an 'anonymous caller'."

"Angus called when you were outside," said Travis. "He said to tell you the print shop in Nimrod was a bust. Nobody remembered the card."

"Great. Our only clue is a business card that can't be traced for a business that doesn't exist."

"There's still the Rumsey print shop."

"Sure. As soon as Angus has time we'll send him over there."

The harsh ringing of the phone on Peter's desk interrupted their conversation and Peter hurried to pick it up.

"Sheriff's office. This is Peter."

"Sheriff. This is Karyn Nichols. I heard a news report on KRUD that said there have been multiple abductions of young women in Anderson and a serial killer is suspected. Why haven't we been informed of this?"

Peter groaned. "That report is completely false as I told the reporters this morning, Mrs. Nichols."

"It can't be false. It was on the news. Why are you withholding information? Was our baby murdered?" She sobbed in near hysteria.

"Mrs. Nichols is your husband home? Mrs. Nichols?"

Uncontrolled sobbing.

"Travis. Could you get Mr. Nichols on the phone?"

"Already done, Boss. I explained everything and he's on his way home."

"You're the best, Travis. Thanks."

At some point Karyn Nichols had disconnected and a dial tone buzzed in Peter's ear.

He heard Birdie ask Travis, "Is it always this chaotic here?"

"No, but we have our moments. Having second thoughts about taking the job?"

"Not at all. This is what I signed up for."

18

MARY SAT AT the bar nursing a drink and a cigarette and watching the local news. Mayor Kalinski and Mavis Vallee were front and center basking in the spotlight.

"Weird about that missing girl," said Eddie, the bartender.

"Yeah, weird," said Mary, her mind going back in time to another missing girl.

Mary had done well for herself in her years at the Roost. The resident band of thugs took the young girl under their wings, unexpected protective instincts coming to the surface. They made sure she ate well and slept well. They insisted she attend school clad in the best clothes to be found in

Anderson. Her protectors weren't equipped to help her with homework, but Mary was a bright girl and grades weren't an issue. High school graduation found Mary with the largest gathering of onlookers than any other student.

Always curious, in her free time between school and work, Mary explored the lot around the Roost and beyond. At the back side of the lot stood an old, neglected house, closed tight from the elements and protected from vandals and looting, but nevertheless, abandoned. It was a small house but built of sturdy red brick with a small attic dormer window and a covered porch in front. Mary had plans for that house. On the eve of her high school graduation, she approached Carl Swenson, the proprietor of the Roost and her unofficial guardian.

"Carl, that old house at the back of the lot, why doesn't anyone live there?"

"It's in pretty bad shape, Mary. I stayed there for a while when I first bought the place, but it needed more work than I wanted to put into it. I'm not the fix-it-up type."

"What kind of work?"

"Well, you know, paint and stuff. Modern appliances. It's probably overrun with mice by now."

"Could I look inside?"

Carl, ever indulgent when it came to Mary, said, "Sure, but be careful. I haven't been in there for years. There could be some weak spots in the floor."

He went into the back office and rummaged through his desk drawer until he found the house key.

"Here ya go. Have fun."

Delighted, Mary gave him a hug and a grin and skipped out the back door.

The lock was stiff, and the wood warped, but with a squirt of oil and persistent jiggling, the door reluctantly swung open, screeching and groaning all the way. Stale dead air flowed out, replaced with a fresh summer breeze. Inside was everything Mary imagined. Worn, but serviceable wood covered the floors, faded French Toile paper coated the walls. A narrow foyer opened into a two large rooms, one each to the left and right, with a stairway in the middle. The rooms were bright in spite of a thick dinge on their bay windows. Mary turned left into what was meant to be a dining room, a dusty area rug still carried the indents from a heavy table. A doorway led Mary back in time to a kitchen furnished with an old-fashioned porcelain gas stove and a Hoosier cabinet.

No wonder Carl didn't stay here.

Behind the kitchen was a utility room complete with a free-standing double sink, broom closet, and pantry. Mary turned a sink handle and was pleased with a strong flow of clear water. Hot water flowed with a turn of the other handle, but the color was rust. Carl had told her the house had a private well with good water.

Maybe needs a new water heater?

She was surprised to find a broom and mop in the closet and several ancient food tins in the pantry.

She made her way back to the foyer and the empty front parlor. A short hallway off the parlor led to a small back porch and a patch of unkempt wild grasses. Two doors opened off the hallway, one to a bathroom and the other a bedroom, both empty of anything but dust. Back in the foyer, the staircase led to a large one-room second floor, fully finished, and filled with an array of antique castaways. A treasure trove of trunks and toys and furniture were waiting to be explored.

Mary laughed out loud, raised her fist in triumph and yelled, "Yes!"

She ran out, front screen door banging behind her, and across the lot to the Roost, surprising Carl as she bounded back into the bar.

"If I clean it out, can I live there?"

"That old house in back?"

"Yes! Yes! Yes!"

"You really want to live in that dusty old place?"

"It's perfect and I'd have a place of my own. Please, Carl?"

He raised one eyebrow. "I did have the roof replaced and the foundation is good."

"Please?" She gave him her best puppy dog face.

"Okay, but wear a facemask when you clean. I don't want you coming down with hantavirus. Who would swamp out the bar?" he teased.

"Like I'm not going to catch something worse cleaning up after this bunch of ruffians."

Mary gave Carl the biggest bear hug she could muster and ran to the storeroom for supplies. She cleaned and polished her new home until it was deemed livable by Carl. The treasure trove of attic antiques were either put to use in the house or sold to finance her project.

Years later, Mary worked keeping the books and ordering supplies while Carl did what he did best, tending bar and schmoozing customers.

One day, Mary found a young girl, lost and alone, sitting in a corner booth at the Roost. *She couldn't be more than fifteen.*

"Are you here by yourself?"

"Um, well, I came here with Wayne. He said he had to see a guy about some business, but that was hours ago." A tear formed at the corner of her eye. "Maybe he got lost on his way back?"

Mary knew better. Someone had found this desperate girl, used her, and dumped her at the Roost.

"Where are you from?"

The girl hesitated.

"Not from around here?" guessed Mary

"Um, no. Back east." She narrowed her eyes. "I'm not going back."

"Anybody looking for you?"

"I doubt it."

"Hungry?"

The girl nodded and the tear spilled onto her cheek. "I haven't eaten for a while."

"Sit tight and I'll grill you a burger."

Mary let the girl eat without talking, refilling her soda when necessary.

As the chewing slowed, she began.

"What are your plans?"

"I was hoping to find a job. I'm a hard worker."

Mary glanced at Carl, who was watching from the bar. He nodded.

"We need someone to clean the bar after hours in exchange for a room and food."

"Really?"

"Your pay is whatever money you find on the floor and tables while you're cleaning."

The girl swallowed and burst into tears of relief. "I'll take it."

Faith was her name and Mary liked the girl. She made sure Faith went to school and helped her with her homework. In the evenings, they ate popcorn and watched movies and shared their hopes and dreams.

And then Faith disappeared, and nobody cared except Mary.

"We can't save them all," said Carl.

"She was happy here, Carl. She wouldn't have left."

"I've seen more than one young girl turn to mush over a smooth-talking guy."

"But she didn't have a boyfriend. She was afraid of men."

Carl shrugged. "You can't save them all Mary."

19

Birdie snapped in her seatbelt and turned to Travis.

"So, where are we going?"

"Well, what would you like to see?"

"Angus showed me the backroads on the outskirts of the county. Let's stay closer to town."

"This probably isn't on your list of fun times, but it's my mom's birthday today. Do you mind if we bring her flowers?"

"What a sweet son. Let's do it."

Travis reached into the back seat and pulled out a bouquet of yellow roses.

"These were her favorite."

"Were?"

"Um, yeah." He started the ignition and turned out of the parking lot. "Have you had a tour of the cemetery yet?"

Anderson's cemetery sat on a pine and fir covered hill on a west slope of the foothills of the Moonlight Mountains. Graves were scattered amongst the trees wherever a large enough space could be found. Travis parked in a clearing at the bottom of the hill and led Birdie along a path into the forest.

"This is different," said Birdie. "I was expecting manicured lawns, rows of headstones, and a chain link fence."

"I guess the miners and ranchers who lived here originally were mostly men. They did what men do and dug a hole and buried someone. None of them wanted to waste good grazing land on a cemetery. By the time the civilized folk got here it was a done deal."

"I like it. It's pretty and peaceful."

Travis led her on a path to a large pink granite headstone engraved in flowers and birds. The name engraved was *Magnolia Berg.*

"She went by Maggie," said Travis.

A vase on a stand filled with faded silk wildflowers was fixed in the ground next to the headstone.

"I leave fake ones most of the time, so she'll always have flowers, but I like to bring real ones on special occasions."

Birdie's heart melted. Now here was a guy she could trust.

"How did she die?" she asked.

Travis looked uncomfortable.

"You don't need to tell me," said Birdie, embarrassed that she'd asked.

"Someday," said Travis. "Someday."

Two large tree stumps lined up alongside the grave site. Travis sat on one and Birdie followed and settled on the other.

"We had to take out two old trees to make room for Mom's plot, but it worked out well for seating options."

They sat silently for a while, breathing in the fresh mountain air, Travis contemplating his mom's death and Birdie contemplating Travis.

"Is your dad still alive?" she asked.

"No, he died before mom. Colon cancer."

"Is his grave here too?"

Travis stood and stretched. "Over here."

He led Birdie around the pink headstone. Back-to-back facing the other direction stood a stone in black granite engraved with trees and mountains.

"They always seemed to be going in different directions in life, so it seemed fitting," said Travis. "Hey, I'm getting hungry. Should we go get something to eat?"

"Sure. I'm kind of hungry too. Where should we go?"

"You've been to The Grill. Dixie's Diner's only open for breakfast and lunch. How about the Silver Dollar Saloon?"

"A bar?"

"Well, kind of. Technically, I guess, but quiet. People go there more for the food than to drink."

"Sounds good." They stood and brushed the grass off their pants.

On the way down the hill to town, Travis snapped out of his thoughts. He glanced shyly at Birdie.

"Thanks for going to the cemetery with me. I know it's not what you were thinking when I said I would show you around."

"Thanks for taking me. It was, well, fun."

Travis laughed. "I know how to show a girl a good time. Seriously, though, I've never brought anyone up there before. It was nice to have company."

The Silver Dollar Saloon was running a midweek special on pulled pork sliders with coleslaw and a side of house chips.

"Sounds perfect," said Birdie.

"Me, too," said Travis and placed their order.

"What do you think happened to Stacey Nichols?" asked Birdie.

"I think she was abducted. She doesn't strike me as someone who would take off without telling her family."

"My thoughts, too. Travis, how long have you been working for the department?"

"Almost three years now."

"Do you know of any other missing persons in that time?"

Travis thought for several minutes.

"Not that I can think of. Are you talking about that press conference? I think that was a publicity stunt by the mayor and Mavis Vallee."

"What if it wasn't?"

"What do you mean?"

"Maybe there have been other missing women. Maybe reports were filed, but they weren't taken seriously."

"I guess it's possible. I mean, we're taking this one seriously because of her close ties to family and friends. She has no history of mental illness. She's stable."

"But what if someone disappeared who was a bit of a wanderer, someone who didn't have family or friends to care if they disappeared. What then?"

Birdie was so intense in her questioning she didn't notice food being delivered and almost knocked hers to the floor. Travis caught the plate in time and moved it to the middle of the table.

"What's going on, Birdie?"

She looked away, lips held tightly closed, eyes filling with tears.

"Birdie?"

Travis reached out and laid his hands over hers and gave them a gentle squeeze.

Birdie turned to face him and sighed.

"I need to tell you the truth."

She told him about college in Missoula and her drinking and the trip to Anderson for the concert in the park. And she told him about Selina. Selina, the odd bohemian girl with her long hair and beads and no one but Birdie to care when she disappeared.

"That's why you went into law enforcement? She's why you wanted to work in Anderson? Do you even care about being a deputy?"

Birdie felt his anger. "No, not only that. Well, at first, but then I went into the program and found out I loved it. And then I came here, and I knew for sure this is where I belong."

Travis pulled his plate over and picked up the first of three pork sliders. He bit, chewed, swallowed, and bit again, not wanting his mouth to be empty long enough for Birdie to expect him to reply. She gathered her knife and fork and cut her slider into small bite-sized pieces before spearing one to eat.

Who eats a slider with a knife and fork? thought Travis.

He wanted to be a deputy. His body building began when he researched the police academy physical requirements. He bought all the books and studied before he'd even been accepted into the program. He graduated the academy with perfect marks and then washed out his first week on the job because no amount of hard work and wishing gave him the needed temperament. Here was a girl who went to school on a whim. Time would tell if she could cut it in the field.

Birdie watched a rollercoaster of emotions ripple across Travis's face.

"Will you help me?" she asked.

Travis downed his second slider before he spoke.

"What happens if we find your friend?"

"What do you mean? I've always assumed she was dead, but at least I would have closure."

"I mean, would you hang up your badge and go back to Birdie the party girl?"

"No, Travis. Those days are long behind me. I've grown up. I don't plan on going anywhere whether we find Selina or not. I'm here for the long haul."

Travis studied her face. Ever since his unfortunate misreading of the situation during the abusive wife incident, he'd been studying how to read people. There were no signs of deceit in Birdie.

"Okay. How do you want to go forward with this? We need to tell Peter."

"Will he be mad?"

"I don't think so."

"I'm okay with investigating off-hours if that's what he wants. Will you help me?"

Of all the ways Travis had imagined spending time with Birdie, investigating a years-old missing vagabond wasn't one. But it was important to her, so it was important to him.

"Sure. Why not. But tracing an uninvestigated disappearance from that many years ago will be near to impossible. This isn't like a cold case you see on TV. There's no file of clues or witness testimonies. The chances of finding someone who even remembers your friend is a long shot. Where would we start?"

"Well, that's the thing. I agree completely. That was a dream I had before studying criminal justice. I get it now. Thinking we could find Selina herself is unrealistic, but what if there are more Staceys and Selinas. What if girls have been going missing for years and nobody noticed because they were girls like Selina who nobody cared about?"

Travis considered. "You mean a serial killer? If there were a history of young girls being murdered in a small town like this, people would know."

"Not if they were from out of town, like Selina, and the killer hid the bodies well. Look around you. We're surrounded by mountains and trees and deep ravines. There must be hundreds or thousands of places that human eyes never see."

Travis followed her line of sight through the window and across the street. A one-room refurbished log cabin filled the lot between towering brick structures. Behind the cabin various homes and businesses stair-stepped up the foothills and beyond. Foothills led to mountains and gaps between mountains opened his view to more mountains.

"You could hide plenty of bodies back there," said Travis. He turned to face Birdie. "Where do we start?"

"Angus told me you've spent gobs of time organizing department records and putting them into the computer system."

"Yeah, records were a mess when I got here. Paper files were shoved in a box and when the box was full, it was stacked on a pile in the basement. Nothing was labeled. Some of it was so damaged from water leaks and mold, I had to throw it out."

"You couldn't have taken pictures of the records before you trashed them?"

"No. The pages were stuck together, and the ink had run. If I couldn't read the pages, I threw them away."

"But you were able to save most of it?"

"Sure."

"How easily accessible are the records in computer files?"

"All cross referenced by victim name, date, status, and type of crime. Easy-peasy."

Birdie beamed in delight and grabbed her purse. "Let's go!" she said, jumping up from her chair.

"Whoa, Nellie," laughed Travis. "Those records aren't going anywhere. Let me finish my dinner."

Birdie looked at him sheepishly and sat back down. "I guess a few more minutes won't make a difference after all these years."

20

Angus left early the next morning for Rumsey. His official excuse for going was to question the print shop about the Flint Creek Valley Bed and Breakfast business card. His real reason was to stop at his parents' house and load his Explorer with personal items to move into his apartment in Anderson. Most things could wait, but he was going to the concert in the park with Holly that evening, and he wanted everything to be perfect. He loaded two deluxe lawn chairs, the recliner style with pull-out cupholders and snack trays.

"Those are your dad's favorite lawn chairs. Are we ever going to see them again?" asked Mrs. McLeod.

"I'll bring them back next week, Mom. You don't want my date sitting on the ground, do you?"

"Of course not. Who is this girl? Is it that new deputy I've been hearing about? The girls at the beauty shop say she's pretty."

"No, Mom. Not her. Can I borrow a cooler, too?"

"I'm not sure what your dad has planned. He may need one if he decides to go fishing."

"He has five of them. I doubt he's going to miss one in the next week."

"Oh, all right," she said, locking him in a tight mama bear hug. "We're sure going to miss you around here."

"I can't live with my parents forever, Mom, and this is a good opportunity."

"Your Uncle Jake won his election. Things might change over there at the courthouse now he's not worried about people thinking you get special treatment."

"I NEVER got special treatment and Uncle Jake is never going to change, Mom. In Anderson I get credit for what I do and not who I am."

"I'm gonna miss you underfoot is all," she said as they made their way back to the garage in search of a cooler. "We hardly see your sister since she got that job in town."

"Char got a job in town? When did that happen?"

Angus's twin sister Char, short for Charolais, had recently declared her intention of running the family cattle ranch when their parents retired. Angus and Char were named after their father's favorite breeds of cattle and Char had the same passion and devotion to raising the breeds.

"I thought she was going to stay on the place and learn the business," said Angus.

"Oh, she is, but she's young and it gets lonely out here. This way she gets into town for socializing and has a little pocket money."

"Where is she working?"

"At that print shop over by the grocery store."

"No kidding." *Well, that should make my investigating easier,* thought Angus.

He finished loading his vehicle, said his goodbyes, and drove into Rumsey. The local grocery store and print shop were midway down Rumsey's main street. Angus turned into the shared parking lot and stopped in front of the print shop.

"Hey, Char," he greeted his twin as he walked in the door.

Char was the same wiry bundle of energy as her brother, the only difference, her blonde locks in contrast to his flaming red.

"Hey, big brother," said Char, born minutes behind her twin. "What brings you to town?"

"An investigation, actually. You might be able to help me."

"Really?! Is it a murder investigation?"

"Only a missing person case so far."

"Oh, okay. What does it have to do with me?"

Angus pulled the business card, protected in a see-through baggie, out of his front uniform pocket.

"Can you tell me anything about this business card?"

"Like, was it printed here?"

"Yeah."

Char studied the card.

"I've never seen it before, but I've only been working here a few weeks. I can tell you if we carry this type of paper."

"Is there anyone here who might remember printing it?"

"I doubt it. The guy who had this job before me was here forever. He retired as soon as he had me trained."

"Sweet. Where can I find him?"

"Down at the coffee shop, about any time of day. He's part of that group of old guys who sit at the corner table and play cribbage all day. Name's Harry. He wears this goofy black and white checked newsboy hat and a bad toupee."

"How do you know it's a bad toupee if he has a hat on?"

Char giggled. "You'll see."

"Uh huh. Can't wait." He waved goodbye and turned toward the door.

"Oh, Angus."

"Yeah."

"Mom called. She said if you stopped in to find out about your new girlfriend."

"You haven't seen me."

Angus walked to the edge of the parking lot and waited for a lone car to pass before crossing the street. A block down, on the far corner, a neon sign in the shape of a coffee cup blinked erratically. Burned out lights caused the cup to appear cracked with coffee leaking out the side. The sign had been on a slow decline for as long as Angus could remember, but the coffee and food inside the shop were good. He pushed the door open, activating a chime. Nobody, including the lone waitress, paid attention to the new arrival. Booths lined the streetside wall under a bank of windows. A long counter dotted with stools stretched the length of the opposite side of the room. Angus wove through tables set haphazardly across the remaining space. Locals had a habit of moving tables and chairs around to suit their needs. In the far corner, he found a group of geriatric men gathered around one large round table. Between each pair was a cribbage board and a scattering of playing cards. Various groans, whoops, and chuckles intermixed with the slap of cards on the table as the men made their plays. They were completely unaware of Angus watching until he cleared his throat.

"Uh, oh, the long arm of the law. Which one of you jaywalked on your way here?" joked a bulging farmer in a faded blue plaid shirt and baseball cap.

"Me actually," said Angus. "Are you going to make a citizen's arrest, Ralph?"

"I'll let you by this time, Angus, but watch yourself."

Chuckles rippled around the table. Angus easily spotted his target amongst the group. A thin, gangly man sat next to farmer Ralph in the described checked newsboy cap. Sticking out of the sides was a pageboy shaped mat in an unnatural black hue. The cap sat sideways on the old man's head, the pageboy mat following the tilt of the cap making Angus wonder if it was attached.

"Harry?" queried Angus.

The man glanced at Angus in surprise.

"Uh, yeah. I'm Harry. Is there a problem, Officer?"

"No problem, but you may be able to help with an investigation. Can we chat outside?"

"Sure." Harry laid the cards in his hand face down on the table and jabbed Ralph on the arm. "No cheating while I'm gone."

He followed Angus out to the sidewalk. Angus pulled the baggie containing the business card out of his pocket and passed it to Harry.

"Char told me you might recognize this?"

Harry studied the card, flipping it back and forth and testing the give of the paper.

"A matte cover stock. We use this style in the print shop, but so does everyone else. The design looks familiar. Can I think on it for a bit?"

Angus pulled another piece of paper out of his pocket. It was a copy of the business card with his cell number written on the back.

"Give me a call if you remember anything."

"Sure thing." Harry folded the paper and buttoned it into his shirt pocket. He stopped to adjust his cap of hair in the reflection from the window before he went back to his game.

Angus crossed the street, got into his vehicle, and looked at his watch. Plenty of time to drive home and clean up for his date with Holly.

Back in his apartment, Angus changed his clothes three times. *Are shorts too casual? A T-shirt and jeans or khakis and a button-down? What will Holly be wearing?* He finally settled for jeans and a light blue button-down oxford. After dressing, he filled the borrowed cooler with ice, an assortment of iced tea and flavored waters, and containers of vegetables and dips for snacking. He had a large bag of potato chips in case Holly was in the mood for junk food. Vendors would be selling plenty of options for dinner.

Angus parked in front of Holly's house and checked his hair in the mirror. No obvious cowlicks so it was a good hair day.

He rang Holly's doorbell and waited patiently for too long. *Is it rude to ring the bell twice? Maybe she's in the bathroom or something and didn't hear it.* He pushed the button again and listened carefully, hearing the chime inside. He waited several more minutes, then glanced at his watch.

Right on time. Did she forget?

A detached garage opened into the alley behind Holly's house. Angus didn't see her car parked streetside so he let himself into the yard through a gate in the white slat fence. A peek in a side garage window verified Holly's car in its usual spot. His stomach did a flip.

Is she inside hurt and unable to answer her door?

He walked back across the lawn and tried the back screen door. Locked. Angus knew that after the recent murder of her Uncle David, Holly started locking her doors, but doubted she would make too much effort to hide the key. He let himself out the gate and studied the area around her front door. No obvious fake rock key holders. He slid his fingers along the ledge above the door. Nothing. He lifted the mat. It needed sweeping, but no key. Not easily discouraged, he continued his search. Next to the bottom step stood a shiny new ceramic garden gnome. Angus picked it up by its peaked cap and looked underneath. Sitting on top of packed dirt was a black plastic key protector. He set the gnome aside, slid open the cover on the box, and tipped the key into his hand. The key was new and stiff, but with jiggling, popped the door lock.

Angus hesitated momentarily, considering the legalities of his actions. Did breaking and entering count if you had a key and it was a friend's house? Legitimate concerns for her well-being tipped him over the edge. Her car was in the garage, and she was supposed to be here. He pushed the door open, calling to Holly as he walked into her foyer.

"Holly? Holly. Are you here? It's Angus."

He searched through the living room and into the kitchen, den, closets, and bathroom on the first floor. Nothing looked out of place. There was no sign of Holly and also no sign of struggle or hurried exits. A single bowl and spoon sat in the sink. A half full cup of coffee sat on the kitchen table. Angus felt the cup. Cold.

Stairs led from the living room to a second floor with three bedrooms and a bath. *Too much room for one person,* thought Angus as he searched the second floor. Holly also owned a large Victorian mansion at the top of Main Street, overlooking the town of Anderson. The mansion had belonged to her Uncle David, and she inherited it when he died. Angus had asked her why she didn't sell this house and move into the mansion. She said every time she walked into the mansion, all she could see in her mind was the blue, lifeless body of her Uncle David hanging from the balcony railing. All Angus could see were rooms filled with red-headed babies. The extensive grounds of the mansion even had a guest house. Angus imagined his mother living there in her waning years, helping to watch over her many grandchildren.

He came back to reality with a start when a cat rubbed against his legs and meowed. He looked down at Holly's fluffy snow-white Persian with the big blue eyes.

"Aren't you kind of a fancy cat for a girl who likes to dig around in the dirt?" he asked.

"Meow."

"Where's Holly?"

"Meow miaow."

"Nice chat."

No signs of Holly in the house, Angus let himself out, carefully locking the door as he left. The second most likely place to look for Holly was The Sapphire Pit. He drove the short distance to her business, convincing himself that she had lost track of time.

Several flocks of tourists were gathered outside The Sapphire Pit, looking annoyed and frustrated that the business wasn't open. Angus was more worried than ever. Where was Holly and where was her partner, Matthew? Even if Holly had the afternoon off, she would have left Matthew in charge.

"Hey, Deputy. What's going on?" asked an overweight lawn chair dad wearing droopy jeans and a bulging T-shirt. "We've drove over specifically to hunt for sapphires."

"Not sure. Is the door locked?" asked Angus as he pushed through the crowd.

"Yep. Nobody around. What a waste of gas and time. I have half a mind to file a complaint with the city."

You have half a mind, period, thought Angus.

"The city has nothing to do with businesses being opened or closed," he said, checking the door for himself.

"What are you going to do about this?" demanded another tourist.

"Look for the owner. In the meantime, find something else to do."

Angus got into his Explorer and drove to the courthouse. He needed to think without a crowd of angry tourists watching. He couldn't get the kidnapped Missoula girl out of his head. Was Holly the next victim? He needed to talk to Peter.

Angus took the courthouse steps two at a time in his rush to report Holly missing now that he knew she wasn't at home or work. Peter's office door was closed, but Angus flung it open without knocking. The room was empty. Angus, in his rush, had forgotten it was Saturday and Peter was off work. He ran back down the stairs, got into his vehicle and punched in Peter's number.

"Hey, Angus, what's going on."

"Peter, it's Holly."

Peter had been lounging in a deck chair at his brother Paul's house. He sat at full attention.

"What's wrong with Holly?"

"She's missing."

Angus explained about their concert plans, Holly's empty house, and the locked Sapphire Pit. Peter was already in his vehicle and on his way to town when Angus finished.

"Do you know if Matt was supposed to be there?" he asked.

"I don't know, but I can't imagine her being closed on a Saturday in the summer. It's her busiest season."

"Meet me at The Sapphire Pit," said Peter and disconnected. Bile rose in his throat.

What happened to Holly?

Peter pulled up to the pit. Angus was already there and pacing.

"Did you try and call her?" asked Peter.

"Yeah, about a dozen times. No answer. It goes straight to voicemail."

"Any reason she would be avoiding your calls?"

"What? No. I talked to her last night. She was excited about the concert."

"Would she have gone by herself?"

"No. She knew I was coming to pick her up."

Peter reached for the door.

"I already tried," said Angus. "Locked."

"Hey," said Peter, "where's the bus?"

"The bus?"

"You know, The Sapphire Pit bus she uses to take people to the dig site."

Angus looked around and then at Peter. "Uh, I didn't think of that. But why would she take the bus up if we were going to the concert. It doesn't make sense."

"Maybe she took it on a morning run. We need to check the route to the mine first. Follow me."

The road to the dig site was narrow, rocky, and slow to drive, one side rising steeply and the other a long straight drop to the valley floor. Both men were in a panic over Holly and short on patience. More than once, Peter heard the clink and scrape of a boulder against his vehicle. Cringing, he reasoned, *sheriff's vehicles aren't supposed to be show pieces.*

Mind occupied with worst case scenario reasons for Holly being missing, he rounded a corner too fast and almost ran into the back of The Sapphire Pit bus. Angus, similarly preoccupied, swerved to miss hitting Peter and skittered on the edge of the road looking down into the deep gulch. Holly, Matt, and a group of tourists came around from the front of the bus, all with relieved smiles.

"Thank goodness!" said Holly as Peter and Angus got out of their vehicles. "There's no phone service up here so we were about to draw straws for who had to walk for help."

Peter looked on in dismay as Angus rushed to Holly and wrapped her in a giant bear hug.

"I was so worried about you," said Angus.

Peter's daydreams of being Holly's rescuing hero were dashed. He was at the same time comforted to know that whatever had stranded the group on the mountain, Matt had not been able to solve the problem. He strode up to Matt, pretending to be unconcerned with the embracing Holly and Angus.

"What happened?" he asked

"I don't know. We were driving along, and the bus died." He looked at Peter sheepishly. "I'm not much of a mechanic."

They watched as Holly pulled a sorting stool out of a rear storage cubby and handed it to Angus. He set it on an even spot in front of the bus and opened the engine compartment.

After only a few moments, Angus closed the hood, wiped his hands on his pants, and said, "Okay, start er' up."

Holly climbed into the driver's seat and turned the key. The engine roared to life to loud cheers and backslaps for Angus.

"We need to learn some mechanicing," Matt whispered to Peter.

"So, what was wrong?" asked Holly.

"A loose battery cable," replied Angus. "It's in bad shape anyway and this rough road finally shook it loose. When's the last time you had this thing into the shop for a tune-up?"

"Um. Well. I make sure the oil is changed when the light comes on."

"Tsk tsk. Don't worry," Angus assured her. "I was raised on farm equipment. I'll get her fixed up for you."

Peter rolled his eyes. "I guess we're both out of the running," he whispered back to Matt.

"I've come to realize I wasn't in the running to begin with. Holly and I are good business partners, but there's no attraction there."

"Really?"

"Yeah, we don't have anything in common other than digging for sapphires and don't even do that for the same reasons."

"Do tell."

"I'm into finding and selling treasure. She's passionate about the geology."

"No kidding. She dumped me because I quit college and took a job in law enforcement."

"So, what does she see in Angus? They have absolutely nothing in common."

"I'm not sure if she realizes they're dating," laughed Peter.

Ten minutes later, the bus was loaded and on its way up the mountain. The narrow road had Angus and Peter also driving to the wide-open dig site to turn around. At the top, everyone agreed they were ready to call it a day. Holly passed out lunches to the group and refunds to her clients.

"I'm sorry, Angus. We'll probably miss the concert," said Holly, biting into a ham and cheese sandwich. "I shouldn't have tried to do a dig this morning."

"No worries. There'll be other concerts," said Angus, still feeling the hero for saving the day and thanking God it was an easy fix.

Later that night, Holly and Angus lounged in his apartment, eating brewery pizza and watching baseball on TV.

Peter was back at Paul and Linda's house settled on a tree stump next to the firepit, watching a brat bubble and hiss on the end of a roasting stick.

"Something changed in you today," observed Paul.

Peter pulled his brat out of the fire and slid it off the stick into a ready-made bun filled with mustard and relish.

"Is it that obvious?"

"You seem more relaxed than you have in a long time."

"All these years I've been hanging onto my past with Holly. I felt guilty if I thought about dating someone else. Like I had to stay faithful to her. When I saw her with Angus today, I realized she had moved on and I was holding myself hostage to the past."

"Welcome back, brother."

21

T HE SUNRISE OVER the mountains was exception-
ally beautiful that morning, as were the many-col-
ored wildflowers dotting the meadow. Stacey sat
staring out the window but was too preoccupied to
notice the scenery. Desperation consumed her. Any
delusions of being released by Ben were long gone.
She would be in that cabin until she died unless she
found a way to escape. Breaking out was impossible.
Despite the difference in their ages, Stacey didn't
have the strength to overpower Ben. She was too
physically damaged. She needed to use her wits and
they were not something she had relied on in her
previously pampered life. Her best chance was to
convince Ben to allow her outside and then escape,

either on foot or in a stolen truck. Did he leave his keys in his vehicle as did so many rural ranchers? Making her way outside would be easy. She would convince Ben to let her help with his porcupines. Escaping after that would be harder. Remembering his setup with the root cellar and barn, she began forming a plan.

Stacey heard tires snapping twigs and scattering rocks. A truck door slammed. A key scraped in the lock. Ben. She never knew if it would be sweet Ben or angry Ben and she felt a trickle of cold sweat run down her back as her hands began to shake in fear.

The door scraped against the wood plank floor as it swung open. Stacey studied Ben's face as he stepped into the room, watching for signs of his mood.

He smiled. "Hi, sweetie. I brought you a special breakfast."

Ben brought a white bakery bag from behind his back and set it on the table.

"Don't look yet. I'll get you a plate."

He walked over and pulled two plates out of the cupboard and tore paper towels off the roll.

"Okay. You can look now," he said as he set a plate and napkin in front of Stacey.

She opened the bag and couldn't help smiling. The aroma of freshly baked sweet rolls was tantalizing even for a prisoner. The bag was filled with an assortment of donuts: raised, cake, glazed, frosted, and filled.

"I drove into town early this morning. The store bakery gives a discount if you get there before seven."

Stacey was conflicted. Here was a man who got up early and drove into town to bring her a special treat. He was also the man who had kidnapped her and broken her wrist and ribs. She was torn between guilt for planning against him and the rational need to escape.

"Pick one, sweetie," said Ben, pulling her out of her thoughts.

"They all look so yummy." She picked a vanilla frosted donut with pink sprinkles.

"I was hoping you would pick that one," said Ben. "It reminded me of you."

Um, weird. She took a bite. It was delicious. "Oh my. That's the best donut I've ever eaten."

Ben grinned from ear to ear. He opened the bag and took out a maple frosted long john.

"These are my favorite."

Stacey and Ben sat at the table eating until the bag was empty.

Stacey moaned. "I'm stuffed."

Ben patted her arm. "You go lie down and sleep that off. I'm going to feed the porkies."

"No! I mean. I'll come with you. I need to walk off all that sugar."

"Sure, sweetie. If that's what you want."

Ben picked up the plates, brought them to the sink, and threw the paper in the trash.

"Well, let's go," he said, motioning Stacey to follow him out.

Stacey took a deep breath, clearing her thoughts and calming her nerves. An overdose of sugar was not the best way to begin a stealth operation, but at least it would give her extra energy. She followed Ben along the path that led to the porcupine barn, wishing that she had thought to ask for pain medication before they left the cabin. With each step, her wrist throbbed and her ribs screamed in pain. When they got to the root cellar, Ben unlatched the door and turned to Stacey.

"You look tired, sweetie. Why don't you stay out here and rest while I load the wheelbarrow?"

"Sure. Thanks."

Perfect, she thought. *Thank you, God*

Ben pulled the door open. Stacey watched as he lifted the lantern off the hook on the inside wall and turned it on with a push of a button. She watched as he lifted the handles of his wooden pushcart. He took one last look behind him before he rolled the cart further into the root cellar.

Stacey rushed to push the door closed and fastened the latch. She heard Ben call out in astonishment and then anger. A rush of adrenaline masked her pain as she stumbled down the path and back to the cabin. She ran straight for Ben's pickup truck and wrenched the door open, collapsing against the seat in frustration when she realized there were no keys in the ignition. She didn't know how far she was from town, but at least there was a road to follow, and each painful step would bring her closer to home.

Her determination was no match for the weakness of her injured body. A fair distance down the road, she saw a large stump and set her goal. "Only for a few minutes," she said to no one as she dropped onto the stump. Her dry throat clenched with the effort and her tongue felt swollen. She longed for moisture, but the roadside was devoid of a creek or even dew on the grass. In her imagination, she heard a car motor. The engine noise grew louder, and she realized it was real. The noise was coming down the hill, around a corner and heading toward town. A car. She pushed herself onto shaky legs with her one good hand and took a few steps closer to the road. She couldn't let it go by without seeing her. As she watched, her heart filled with dread. It wasn't a car. It was a truck. A red truck just like Ben's. She could see his angry insane face through the windshield. Her mind told her to run, but her legs were paralyzed with fear. She fell to the ground and sobbed as she heard the truck grind to a stop, road gravel scattered by the tires pelting her skin. The door opened and Ben leaped out.

"You stupid, stupid girl," he yelled as he kicked her already broken ribs. "Did I forget to tell you about the back door?"

He grabbed her by a leg, bouncing her head along the gravel as he drug her to the rear of the truck, letting go long enough to unlatch the tailgate. He clasped onto a clump of her hair in one hand and the waist band of her skort and swung her into the bed of the pickup. Relieved of consciousness by pain and fear, Stacey was unaware of her body tumbling in the back of the truck as it made its way up the steep mountain.

Her next conscious moment found her on the ground at the edge of a dark cavern and the last thing she saw was the sole of Ben's boot as he shoved her into the pit.

22

"N o, MAVIS, WE don't have any leads on the missing girl. You'll be the first to know."

"Yeah, right," said Peter to himself as he disconnected the call.

Thanks to Mavis and the mayor and their publicity seeking press conference, the entire area was in a panic. Missing person reports flooded the sheriff's office. Every call had to be taken seriously and, so far, every suspected missing person was found exactly where they were supposed to be. Peter was thankful for Travis. His years dealing with Mavis and the mayor were perfect training for dealing with an irrational public.

An unfamiliar gruff voice echoed in the hallway and Peter braced himself for the next onslaught.

"You have a visitor, Peter," said Travis from his doorway.

Behind him stood a grizzled old seaman with a grin on his face.

"Preston Clairmont! Stony! What brings you to Anderson?" said Peter, standing to shake the old sailor's hand.

Stony Clairmont had lived for years on a boat in a shallow harbor on the back side of Georgetown Lake.

"Rheumatism and a generous aunt convinced me to move into town. I sold that rusty old trawler to a young buck with more romantic notions than common sense."

"A generous aunt? Someone here in town?"

"Ida Clairmont. She passed on this last winter."

Peter remembered the gruesome discovery by concerned neighbors of Ida's quickly thawing corpse. He hadn't made the connection with Stony.

"The autopsy showed she froze to death. There were no injuries other than skinned knees from falling down with an armful of firewood."

"That's what I'm told," said Stony. "She was a tough ol' bird. That cabin she lived in was no morn' a prospector's hut. Insulation was old newspapers tacked to the walls."

"You sold your boat for that?" asked Travis, who was listening from the other room.

"No, for the land. Ten acres and a gold mine. The hut isn't much better n' a tent, but I can stand it for the summer. I'm having a cottage built, running water, 'lectricity and all."

"Good for you," said Peter. "And great to see you again. Anything we can do for you?"

"Naw, came into town for groceries and thought I'd stop by and say hello."

Angus poked his head in the door. "Hey, Boss. I got a call back from the guy in Rumsey who printed that business card for the bed and breakfast."

Peter motioned him in. "Anything worthwhile?"

"Yeah. He remembers printing those particular cards because he didn't recognize the Flint Creek Valley Bed and Breakfast. When he asked about it, the guy he printed them for acted nervous, threw some cash on the counter, grabbed his cards and left."

"Did he have a description?"

"Old guy. In his seventies maybe. Gray hair. Looked like a farmer."

"Not much to go on, but at least we know we're looking for an old farmer."

"Is this about that missing girl I've been hearing about?" asked Stony, standing to make his exit.

"Yeah. That business card is our only clue."

"I'll keep an eye out."

Travis called from the other room, "The hospital phoned for an assist with a psych patient."

Angus headed for the door

Peter grabbed his hat and whistled to Zack. "Hold on and I'll come with you."

He was surprised to see Birdie walking up the stairs.

"Weren't you on shift with Helen last night?"

"Um, yeah, uh, well, Travis was going to show me how to do records searches today."

Angus was already halfway down the stairway, so Peter hurried to catch up, wondering what Birdie and Travis were really up to.

Expecting to walk into the typical chaos of a psych assist, Peter and Angus were surprised to find Dr. Hamm, handsome and beloved local doctor, sitting quietly next to the hospital bed, calmly chatting with the patient while he cleaned and stitched a hand wound. Nancy May, sporting a chic wig and stylish blouse with matching skirt and heels, stood next to the hospital bed.

The patient was Iris Moon, local character, and possible schizophrenic. Iris watched the stitching with fascination while her friend and protector, Nancy May, stood over the doctor critiquing his work.

"The third stitch is a bit crooked, Dr. Hamm," observed Nancy. "Will that make the scar crooked?"

"I believe that happened when you were rationalizing the inferiority of snakes to spiders as pets. And the scar will be crooked regardless, Nancy. It was a jagged wound. I had to cut away quite a bit of tissue."

"If Iris had stepped on a spider, she would have squished it rather than falling and cutting her hand on the edge of that cupboard. And spiders can't eat you for breakfast."

"Nancy's right, Iris," said Dr. Hamm. "There have been cases of pet boa constrictors killing their owners or escaping and killing someone else. Having a snake crawling around loose in your apartment isn't safe. I'm surprised the complex management allows it."

"Why do you have a boa constrictor in your apartment, Iris?" asked Peter.

Noticing the sheriff and his deputy in the room for the first time, Iris's bug eyes, magnified by the thick lenses in her cat-eye glasses, widened in fear. Paired with her wild unkempt gray hair it wasn't hard to understand the rumors of mental illness. "Am I in trouble for having a snake, Sheriff?"

Peter pulled up a stool next to Iris and patted her shoulder. "Pet snakes aren't illegal in Montana, Iris. I was just curious."

"It's all because of old Mr. Darby. I sat there at his bedside holding his hand as he died and promised him I would take care of his snake." She studied Peter's face for understanding. "There he was taking his last breaths and all he cared about was that snake. What else could I do?"

"Understandable, but whether Mr. Darby is singing praises or shoveling coal, I doubt his main concern at this point is that snake. I'm sure we could find a more suitable home."

"Besides," said Nancy, "you promised you would take care of his snake. You didn't say you would do it personally."

Iris looked at Nancy hopefully. "So, it wouldn't be a lie if I found it a good home?"

"Not at all, unless you like living with a creepy reptile that would kill you in your sleep."

"The truth is that thing gives me the creeps. My kitties won't come out of the bedroom. I spend most of my time in there with the door closed and locked." Iris stifled a sob. "I don't know how much longer I can live like this."

Nancy patted her arm. "Peter is going to call Rick at animal control right now to catch that snake." She gave Peter her best stink eye stare. "Aren't you, Peter."

Peter laughed. "Rick still mad at you over the skunk, Nancy?"

"Humph. Yes, he has me blocked on his cell phone and won't answer when I call the office. Why is it my fault he let a skunk loose in the courthouse?"

"No worries. We'll have that snake taken care of before you get home, Iris."

Iris's sobs turned to tears of relief. "Oh, thank you so much, Peter."

Nurse Kelly, sitting silent at the nurse's station, cleared her throat to catch Peter's attention. "Could I talk to you for a minute," she asked.

"Sure." He turned to Angus. "Could you call Rick and have him take care of that snake?"

Angus pulled out his cell phone and went into the hallway to make the call.

Peter took the chair next to Kelly. "What's going on?"

Kelly put a finger to her lips and pushed a cherry-blossom pink, hobo-style purse toward Peter. "This is the purse Iris came in with."

Baffled, Peter said, "And… ?"

"She told me I could take her wallet out for insurance information to register her into the emergency room."

Kelly reached into the purse, took out a hot pink leather wallet, and handed it to Peter. "Look inside."

Peter unclasped the wallet and opened it to reveal several card slots and a driver's license window. He gasped in surprise when he scanned the driver's license picture and read the name. *Stacey Nichols. 365 Ponderosa Avenue, Missoula, Montana.* Peter looked at Kelly, then back at Iris and to Kelly again.

"Did you ask her about this?"

"No. I recognized the name and picture as the girl who went missing. That's why I called you."

"I thought it was about the snake."

"I didn't even know about the snake until you got here. I looked through the rest of the purse and it definitely belongs to Stacey Nichols."

Peter collected his thoughts for a few moments and then walked back to the bedside and sat and thought some more.

He cleared his throat. "Iris."

"Yes, Peter."

"Iris. Nurse Kelly showed me your purse."

Iris looked confused. "Yes. It's a nice one isn't it. I found it at the thrift store. People donate the nicest things."

"The thrift store here in town?"

"Yes. Last month when I got my social security check. I had a few dollars left over after paying the bills," said Iris defensively.

"I'm not worried about how you spend your money, Iris. I'm sure you're very frugal. I'm interested in the purse."

"They only had the one, but if you looked, I'm sure they have something else as nice."

"No, Iris, I'm not interested in buying a purse, I'm interested in where you got that one and how long you've had it."

"I told you, Peter, I got it at the thrift store last month. Are you feeling okay? You sure are acting strangely."

Lord give me strength for little old ladies, prayed Peter.

Peter walked over to the nurse's station, picked up the purse and brought it back to the bedside.

"Are you sure this is your purse, Iris?"

"Of course, it's my purse. Whose else's would it be?" said Iris, tired and annoyed.

"Please look at it closely."

Iris picked up the purse and held it next to her binocular glasses. "It looks like my purse. I remember that pretty color."

"Let me see," said Nancy.

Iris handed her the purse and Nancy scrutinized every detail.

"I was with you when you bought that purse, Iris, and this one isn't even the same style. The one you bought was a quilted shoulder bag. Very classy. This is something a younger person would use."

She moved to hand the purse back to Iris, but Peter intercepted and took it instead.

"Iris. This isn't your purse. The wallet inside has a driver's license and other items that belong to someone else."

"What? What do you mean? How could that be?"

"That's what we need to find out. When was the last time you used your purse?"

Iris thought. And thought.

"You know," said Nancy. "It was probably when we went to the senior special at the brewery on Tuesday."

"They have a senior special at the brewery?" said Angus in disbelief.

"Well, yes, Angus," retorted Nancy. "We don't all sit around crocheting Afghans and watching game shows."

"It's a nice spread," said Iris. "And we get half-price beer if we buy the lunch buffet." She leaned over and whispered to Peter, "I always bring a ziplock baggie and fill it with goodies before I go."

"Would you have put that baggie in your purse?"

"Oh, no. I did that once and it leaked all over. What a mess. I had to wash out the dollar bills and hang them on the clothesline. Tuna salad soaked into everything. That purse got thrown out."

"When was the last time you opened your purse?"

"Probably when I paid for the buffet."

"What did you do with your purse after that?"

Iris thought. "I set it next to my chair like I always do."

"Do you remember who was sitting at the table next to you?"

Iris thought. And thought.

"It was an older gentleman and a young lady," said Nancy. "I thought it was sweet she was out with her grandfather."

"Could you identify her if you saw a picture?"

"Maybe. I remember she was very pretty with long wavy blonde hair."

"What about the older gentleman?"

"Well, you know, they all look alike unless they have something distinguishing like a huge honker of a nose."

"Did anything stand out about this guy."

"No. Ordinary. Gray hair. Medium height. Medium build. What's this all about, Peter?"

"The purse you were carrying belongs to a missing young woman. We believe she was at the brewery before she disappeared. You two may have been the last people to see her and somehow, Iris, you and she switched purses."

Peter opened the purse, took out Stacey Nichols's driver's license, and showed it to Iris and Nancy.

"Is this the girl who was sitting at the next table?"

They both studied the photograph.

"Um, maybe," said Iris, looking to Nancy for assurance.

"Yes," said Nancy. "Yes, I believe that is the same girl."

"Did you leave first or did they?"

"I'm not sure. I wasn't paying attention to them after we got our food."

"So, you didn't notice them walking to or from a particular vehicle?"

"No. Sorry." She turned to her friend. "This is so exciting, Iris. We're assisting with an investigation. Are you going to deputize us, Peter?"

"Not yet, Nancy, but I'd appreciate if you both think over that day and try and remember anything that would help in our investigation."

Nancy beamed. Iris looked worried. Typical of the opposites, Nancy was ready for adventure and Iris was stressed by anything out of the ordinary.

Peter and Angus left Nurse Kelly to finish with Iris and drove back to the sheriff's office, pink purse safely sealed in an evidence bag. They found Travis and Birdie, heads together, deep in concentration.

"What are you two studying so hard?" asked Peter.

They both looked up with guilty faces.

"Just searching through old missing person cases," said Birdie. "We're checking to see if any are unsolved."

"Hmmmm. Looking for a serial killer?"

Travis stared at Birdie, willing her to confide in Peter about her friend Selina. She chose to ignore his cue.

After a moment, Peter said, "Good police work. We can't rule anything out. Right now, we have an update on the Stacey Nichols case you two need to hear."

Birdie and Travis put aside their notes and followed Angus and Peter into his office. Peter sat behind his desk and the others choose various spots on the worn, but comfortable leather couch and chairs scattered around Peter's office. Peter laid the pink purse on his desk.

"Iris Moon walked into the emergency room this afternoon needing a few stitches. Nurse Kelly asked her for an insurance card and Iris handed her this purse and told her she could find the card in her wallet. Kelly instead found a wallet belonging to Stacey Nichols, including a driver's license and other personal belongings."

"You're kidding," said Travis. "Do you think Iris had something to do with Stacey's disappearance?"

"No. She had no idea it wasn't her purse. It turns out she and Nancy May were at the brewery on Tuesday. Iris is a bit foggy, but Nancy described a young woman with long wavy blonde hair sitting with an older gentleman at the table next to them. I showed her Stacey's driver's license and she agreed that it was the same woman."

"So, how did Iris end up with Stacey's purse?"

"She said she always sets her purse next to her chair. Maybe Stacey does the same and one or the other of them grabbed the wrong purse when they left. There's not much room and those tables are pushed fairly close together. The purses were basically the same color."

"Did they remember anything else?"

"The older man was nondescript. Gray hair, medium height, medium build. Nancy assumed it was the woman's grandfather."

"Basically the same description we got from the print shop."

"Yep. I told Nancy to give us a call if she remembered anything else. I'm not holding up much hope for Iris."

"Anything interesting in the purse?" asked Birdie. "Maybe Stacey purposely switched the purses because she was being abducted."

Peter studied Birdie, impressed with her investigative instincts. He pulled a pair of nitrile gloves out of his pocket and glanced at Birdie.

"My prints and Nurse Kelly's are already all over it... along with Nancy and Iris's, but no use making it worse. We'll check for other prints later. Let's have a look."

He opened the evidence bag, pulled out the purse, unzipped the various internal and external pockets, then emptied the contents onto his desk, Besides the wallet, there was a mini brush, lipstick, a compact, coin purse, gum, nail clippers, and a cell phone.

"Sorry, Birdie. No notes with *HELP* written in lipstick, but that was a great idea."

"Now we know why she wasn't answering her phone," said Travis.

Peter picked up the phone and pushed the power button. "It's dead. Does anyone have a charging cable that will fit this phone?"

"I do," said Birdie. "It's the same brand as mine."

Peter handed her the phone. "As soon as it has enough power, go through it and see if you come up with anything interesting. She may have left a clue on her phone."

"Got it." Birdie took the phone into the other room, where her phone charger was plugged into the wall.

Peter rubbed his temples. "I'm stuck. We have a pretty good idea Stacey was taken by an elderly nondescript man but have no clue how to find them. Any thoughts?"

Crickets.

Angus studied his fingernails. Travis found a sudden fascination with his shoelaces.

"Has Helen been in yet?"

"No, but I'll update her when she checks in," said Angus, "and see if she has any ideas."

"So, what are you and Birdie working so hard on, Travis?" asked Peter.

"Birdie," called Travis, "let's show Peter what we've found."

Birdie walked in and stood next to Travis, who laid a file folder of printouts on Peter's desk. "First, we pulled all the records of missing person reports and eliminated the closed cases. Most of them were resolved within the first day. People panicking because someone didn't answer the phone or took too long coming back from the store. Some of them were eventually found deceased, lost in the woods or drowned, that sort of thing. Then we separated by gender. In the last ten years, ten women have been reported missing, always young women, always at the same time of year. Stacey Nichols is the first one who had family concerned about her disappearance."

"Any guesses on the others, why the cases were dropped?"

"They were all transient types, possibly prosti-tutes, bar flies, the type of people who leave town in the night without paying their bills. Police reports were filed in an effort to recover rent money or bar tabs. The filers didn't care about the missing people otherwise," said Travis.

"Let me guess," said Peter, "everything on the lease agreements was false and the landlords hadn't bothered to do a background check."

"Exactly, but these are slumlords anyway. Tenants were usually folks down on their luck. Sometimes the landlord got paid, sometimes they didn't, but they weren't out much."

"Interesting. Stacey Nichols is the outlier. What does she have in common with the other girls?"

"The time of year. All the other girls disappeared mid-July."

"What else did the other girls have in common besides being transient and going missing around the same date?"

"Nothing yet, but we're still going through the files."

Travis's desk phone jingled.

23

"I'M TELLING YOU this in confidence, Travis," said Mabel in a voice that dared him to argue.

"Sure, what do you have?"

"I remembered a couple who live south of town. They have one of those rambling old farmhouses with six or seven bedrooms."

"Okay."

"This is between you and me, right?"

Travis sighed. "What does this involve, Mabel?"

"You were asking me about bed and breakfasts listed with the Chamber of Commerce. This one isn't. It's kind of 'under the table' if you know what I mean."

Making money off the radar of the IRS wasn't unusual. "I get it. So, these people rent out rooms in their house?"

"They don't advertise or anything. It's word of mouth. Nothing fancy, but clean and good food… and down in Flint Creek Valley. It might be worth checking out."

"Wow, thanks, Mabel. Do you have an address?"

"I don't, but I can give you directions." She rambled off a convoluted set of instructions including barns that had burned down decades earlier and families long since dead.

Travis rolled his eyes. "Got it. How about a name?"

"Can't do that. And don't you dare tell them I sent you!"

"Thanks, Mabel. I owe you one." *And I'll probably regret saying that.*

He disconnected and jumped up from his chair.

"Peter! We have a lead." He filled Peter in on the unofficial bed and breakfast.

Peter lifted his token Stetson off its hook. He whistled to Zack and said, "Come on, Angus. Let's go check this place out."

Peter had lived in Stone County long enough to understand Mabel's vague directions and it didn't take him long to find the sprawling two-story ranch house. Like many homes in the west, wings had been added as the family grew and this had been a large family.

"How are we going to approach this?" asked Angus.

"Best case scenario, we find the kidnappers. Be prepared for a fight. Worst case scenario, they're a nice couple bringing in extra money to make ends meet."

"That seems backward."

"Welcome to law enforcement." He looked over at Angus as he pulled up to the house. "You go around back. I'll take the front."

Peter parked under a large willow tree, providing Angus cover to slip to the back of the house. A well-kept lawn led to a roomy front porch, where several rocking chairs and a porch swing sat idle. The entry door, painted a cheery blue to match the window shutters, sat ajar, the opening guarded by a screen door. Scents of warm baked goods drifted on the breeze. Peter's stomach growled. He tapped lightly on the screen door and was rewarded with a "coming" and light footsteps from inside the house.

"Well, hello, Sheriff," said a middle-aged woman Peter recognized as a regular at community events. She pushed open the door and stepped aside to let Peter through, giving Zack an ear scratch.

His hopes for rescuing Stacey Nichols wavered. Unless the woman was married to a much older man, she was in the wrong age category for the kidnapper. He searched his memory for a name.

"Mrs. Harris, isn't it?" asked Peter.

"Shelly. Is everything okay?"

Visits from Peter were generally met with two predominant reactions. Crooks were hostile or scared. Innocent folks tended to expect bad news about a loved one. Shelly's reaction told Peter she was likely in the latter category.

She led Peter through the front room and into a large airy kitchen painted in orange and cream. Loaves of freshly baked bread lined the counter flanked by pans of cinnamon rolls.

"I have a booth at the farmers' market on Saturdays. Home-baked goods do well with the tourists."

Peter swallowed rather than drooling, Zack was not so polite.

"Would you like a cinnamon roll, Sheriff? I always make extra for the family."

"Yes, I would, thanks. They smell delicious."

Peter sat at the table and watched as Shelly expertly scooped a cinnamon roll out of a pan and onto a plate. She set it in front of him with a fork and napkin and took the chair opposite.

As Peter pressed the side of his fork into the roll, it oozed butter and icing. He was so engrossed in his first bite, he didn't notice Shelly had stopped chattering about the farmers' market.

"There's a strange man peeking in the window!" she exclaimed.

Peter dropped his fork and turned to follow her gaze. An inch of curly red hair poked over the windowsill.

"Hold on," said Peter. He walked to the back door and leaned out. "Angus. You can come in now."

"What's going on, Sheriff?" asked Shelly as Angus came in the door.

"I apologize, Shelly," said Peter. "We're here on an investigation. We only had an address. We didn't know whose house we were coming to. This is my deputy, Angus McLeod."

"Oh. All right. Well, make yourselves comfortable, I guess. Angus, would you like a cinnamon roll?"

"Um, yeah, that would be great. Thanks."

While Shelly prepared a roll for Angus, Peter cleared his throat.

"We had a report of a bed and breakfast at this address, Shelly. Do you know anything about that?" asked Peter.

Shelly turned, spatula in hand, and a surprised look.

"Is that what this is about? A few guests now and then?"

"Do you run a bed and breakfast?" asked Peter.

"Not really. Now and then when there's something big going on in town and the motel is full, we take in overflow. Friends of friends. That sort of thing. We have so many extra bedrooms, it made sense. We don't charge a fee so much as people leave what they think is fair. I call it my fun money. Are we in trouble with the IRS?"

"We don't work for the IRS, Shelly. This is part of a criminal investigation. Do you have a name for your business?"

"No. It's not a business. We take in extras now and then. That's all."

In her flustered state, Shelly forgot about Angus's cinnamon roll. He eyed Peter's.

Peter took the Flint Creek Valley Bed and Breakfast card out of his pocket and handed it to Shelly.

"Have you ever heard of this?"

She read the card. "No. It's definitely not us and I haven't heard of another place by that name around here."

"How do your guests find you?"

"My husband, Steven, goes into town and picks them up."

"How does he know where to find them?"

"I don't know. I guess the motel calls him. That's his thing. I take care of the cooking and cleaning."

A group of family photos were displayed above a secretary desk on the far wall. Peter stood and studied the pictures. He recognized Shelly in several with a dark-haired man about her age.

"Is this your husband?" he asked.

"Yes, that's Steven."

"Only two of you living here?"

"Yes. We don't have any guests at the moment."

"Is he home?"

"Steven? No. He builds houses. He's on a project east of town."

Steven wasn't the gray-haired elderly man suspected of kidnapping Stacey Nichols. Peter, disappointed in the dead end, donned his hat and motioned to Angus and Zack.

"I'm sorry we interrupted your day, Shelly. We obviously received false information, but we need to follow up on every tip."

"I understand, Sheriff. I hope you find your bad guy."

As Angus scooted around the table, he grabbed Peter's napkin and folded it around the cinnamon roll. When they were back in the Explorer, he opened the napkin and started to take a bite.

"Is that my cinnamon roll?" asked Peter.

Angus couldn't hide his guilty face. "Uh, yeah."

"At least give me half. I didn't even get a taste."

Angus split the roll down the middle and handed half to Peter, who tossed a bite to Zack.

"We should stop by more often on farmer's market day."

"I think she'd catch on after a while."

24

Dust came off the blanket in a cloud. *Have I had that mirror covered for that long?* thought Helen.

She remembered the day she put the blanket over the mirror, the day Ray had packed and gone, and Helen opened her first pint of ice cream. She ate until she hurt, but the pain distracted from the ache in her heart.

Now she studied herself frontways and sideways. Only a few days of dieting and exercise and she could swear her buttons strained less in the widest places. The new chic haircut distracted people from looking down so that was a plus. And then there was Adam. He seemed to like her the way she was.

Helen had the beautiful Birdie to thank for the new look and new outlook on life, yet she was uneasy about the coming nightshift. *Birdie. Was I that young and innocent once?* In spite of the initial competitiveness and jealousy, Helen was feeling like a mother hen protecting a chick. *And to think Peter was worried about the guys being protective of Birdie.* Helen thought about the mean drunks and the strung-out druggies and the backwoods kooks protecting their stills. *Is Birdie ready?*

⸻⸻•◦•●•◦•⸻⸻

BIRDIE WAS LOOKING forward to another night shift. Helen had so much knowledge gleaned from decades of experience, and she was willing to pass that knowledge on in a way the guys couldn't, with the understanding of a woman.

Rather than both of them driving across town to meet at the courthouse, Helen picked Birdie up at The Sapphire Inn.

"Any luck finding an apartment?" she asked as Birdie climbed into the Explorer and buckled her seat belt. "It's got to get old living in the motel."

"It is, but I haven't had time to do much looking yet. Work's been busy and by the end of the day I'm bushed."

"Are you thinking about buying a house?"

"Eventually. I'm on probation for a year and still have to go through the police academy."

"While we're on patrol tonight, we'll drive by a few rental possibilities. The apartment complexes usually have phone numbers posted. There's a nice one on East Summit."

"Gee, thanks!"

"Hey, you're part of the team now. We watch out… whoa!"

Helen slammed on the brakes as a body rolled off the hood of a parked car and into the street in front of them. Several dark figures followed, persisting in the brawl and unaware of the sheriff's vehicle. Her practiced spiel to Birdie about staying out of the action until she graduated from police academy was forgotten as Helen spilled out of the Explorer.

Shots were fired and Helen felt the sting of a bullet grazing her arm before she heard Birdie yell, "Police, drop your weapon."

Helen dropped to the ground and rolled behind the front tire.

The sounds of thumps, moans, cursing and the scattering of feet on pavement were followed by, "Cool it, dirtbag." Birdie again. "You're not going anywhere but jail."

Helen rolled to a sitting position and dared a look around the edge of the tire. The street and sidewalk were deserted except for Birdie and a still cursing hoodlum, cuffed and face down on the pavement. Birdie was confidently informing the criminal of his Miranda rights.

"Let's get him back to the station and you'll get your first lesson in writing up a report," said Helen, standing to assist Birdie. "Although I have a feeling you've been practicing that, too."

Back at the sheriff's office, the prisoner booked and jailed, Birdie examined the bullet wound on Helen's arm.

"You're right. It ruined your shirt, but it's only a scrape."

"I'll have to go in and get it checked out anyway. Protocol." She tossed Birdie her keys. "Here. You drive. My arm hurts."

On the way to the hospital, Helen said, "Okay, tell me what happened back there."

"Let me think. It all happened so fast. You bailed out and I saw the guy with the gun. He was pointing to the group on the ground, but when he heard the car door open, he aimed the gun at you. By that time, I was out and had my weapon drawn, and yelled for him to drop his weapon. I don't think he heard me because he fired at the same time. I couldn't shoot into the crowd, so I holstered and got out my taser and ran over and tased him. I cuffed him and then you were there. Wow! What a rush."

"I am impressed, Birdie. You kept your cool in an intense situation."

"Thanks, Helen. Wow!"

Helen laughed. "Most rookies would still be shaking."

"Hey, what was that place anyway?" asked Birdie.

"Where we ran into the group of thugs?"

"Yeah."

"Rustler's Roost. That place gives seedy bars a bad name and on purpose. It started out as a hole-in-the wall hangout for cattle rustlers and folks called it as they saw it. The nickname stuck. It's still a hangout for every kind of dirtbag and they wear the name like a badge of honor."

"Can't we shut them down?"

"I wish. The owners are pretty good at staying ahead of the law. We've tried to get them for serving minors, but they don't. The liquor license is always up to date. We know there's drug business going on, but we haven't been able to catch them."

"Hmmmm," said Birdie. "Rustler's Roost. That name sounds familiar."

"It's popular with the low-lives and hated by the holier-than-thous and most decent folk in between. You probably heard someone mention it in the grocery store."

"Maybe," said Birdie.

A dab of antibiotic cream and a Band-Aid, and Helen was deemed fit for duty by a frazzled ER doc.

"I've spent the last hour stitching and taking X-rays of that bunch of brawling hoodlums you ran into outside the Rustler's Roost."

"The one who shot me was probably the instigator and he's going to be locked up for a while," said Helen.

"So, I might get some sleep tonight?"

"You can always hope."

Helen and Birdie drove back to the Rustler's Roost in an attempt to glean information about the brawl out of the remaining patrons. As usual, nobody saw a thing.

25

Bone-numbing cold and the soul-crushing darkness of a cave at night met Stacey when she woke. Her own shrill scream stifled the panic. It hurt too much. Her head throbbed and bones shrieked. New wounds joined the old. Silent tears were the compromise. Eventually, tears spent, she drew in a deep shuddering breath and willed herself to think.

I'm not dead. I will not die.

That's what she told herself, but a saner place in her brain told her she most likely would die a slow painful death in that dark damp pit. She heard the shuffle of rodent feet and bit down on her lips, knowing the pain brought by a scream. Would rats eat her alive or wait until she died to begin gnawing her flesh? She wouldn't have the strength to push them away.

Her repressed scream turned quickly to laughter as she felt the bristly quills of a porcupine brush against her arm and wet flesh tickling her skin.

A tongue? Is the porcupine licking me?

There was no fear in this. She knew porcupines were herbivores. Her time with Ben taught her that. She felt more small bodies surround her and heat from those bodies brought her comfort. She had no answer to why they were in the cave, but their presence had a calming effect. She was not alone.

Warmth brought strength and with strength came resolve and clarity of thought. The porcupines were not trapped in the cave, or they wouldn't have survived. She felt the ground around her body. Dirt, rocks, and branches of various sizes littered the floor of the cave, damp in places, but not wet. She rolled sideways, away from the broken ribs, and pushed herself to a sitting position with her good wrist. The porcupines, undisturbed by her movement, adjusted and curled back against her legs and back.

Stacey sat motionless and felt for the movement of air against her skin. Somewhere in her memory she knew that trick, maybe from a book she'd read. Air current would lead her to an opening into the cave. The lack of current from above reinforced her suspicions that climbing out the way she came in, via boot down a steep narrow pit, was not an option. The air against her face was also devoid of movement. She felt a twinge of disappointment and fear. Was the air current story only an urban myth?

If you give up, you'll die.

Stacey swung her legs around and pushed herself onto her knees. A sharp pain in her left ankle told of yet another injury and one more obstacle in her fight for life. Despair was not an option. The pain in Stacey's ankle made her angry.

I will live if I have to crawl out of this cave on my hands and knees, well, one hand.

Turning to the side, she felt a gentle draft against her cheek.

There it is.

Attempting to move into the draft, Stacey realized the delusion in her determination. Even the smallest rock grinding against a knee brought unbearable pain. Balancing on a single wrist and pushing herself forward with one foot was beyond her abilities. She needed a crutch. Crouching on her knees, and ignoring occasional lumps of indeterminate goo, she swept her hand in ever widening circles along the rocky ground, willing a suitable stick to find its way into her grasping hand. Her fingertips brushed against a rise in the floor. Scooting closer, she moved her hand along the incline and met resistance. A wall. Piles of debris cluttered the edges giving Stacey hope. Fumbling, her fingers growing stiff and numb from the cold, her hand was temporarily caught in something soft and pliable. She shuddered, imagining what sort of creature had left its fur lying at the edge of the cave. Underneath, her fingers bumped against something of more substance and her hand grasp a possible cane, long and round, but not enough.

Tree branches washed down in spring rains? she thought. *There must be more.*

Her excitement grew as she found an even longer and sturdier piece trapped in the debris. A sharp tug dislodged the stick, flinging the rubble on top into Stacey's lap. She heard something round drop and roll onto the ground in front of her and curiosity brought her hand to feel. Fingers fit into holes in the odd shaped ball, two together and then one below and underneath. Stacey screamed and dropped the ball as she felt teeth firmly anchored in the top half of a jawbone. Flat, even teeth. Realization that the perfect cane she still held in her other hand was most likely a human bone sent her into a spiral of despair.

Her final conscious perception was the warmth of porcupines curling against her and the tickle of their long, licking tongues.

26

THE CONSTRUCTION CREW was off for a three-day holiday. Stony Clairmont had never owned a calendar, so he wasn't sure which one. Days off for the crew meant days Stony didn't have to hang around and supervise and he was running short on groceries.

"Hey, mister," yelled a kid holding court on a metal folding chair, in front of the grocery store.

Stony had a soft spot for kids. He took out his wallet, ready to buy a box of cookies or whatever the kid was hawking.

"What's this?" he said when he realized the cardboard box in front of the kid wasn't full of cookies.

"Pa won't let me keep them all," said the kid. "He said I had to get rid of them or he would, and you know what that means." He nodded with the wisdom of a child and ran a finger across his throat.

A mass of wriggling black puppies yipped and jumped at the sides of the box.

"What sort a' dog are they?" asked Stony.

"Their ma is a cow dog. No tellin' what the dad is. I 'spect it was that ol' shepherd next door."

Stony reached into the box and held his hand steady, testing the temperament of the pups. While most of them nipped and jumped at his hand, one sat in the corner, calmly watching the ruckus. He lifted the pup in one hand and held the other to its mouth. The pup gave him a lick and lifted its snout for approval.

"I'll take this one. How much?"

"Free to a good home, mister."

"Done. What do you call him?"

"Her. I call 'er Lizbeth."

"Lizbeth?"

"Yeah. Ma says the rest a' them are hooligans, but she sets back all regal like a queen."

Stony shifted the pup into the pocket of his elbow and slipped a Jackson off the stack of bills in his wallet.

"Here, son. Buy yer mama somethin' pretty."

"Gee, thanks, mister. I know Lizbeth is goin' to a good home."

Stony contemplated the logistics of a puppy in the grocery store and in the end trusted her aristocratic manners and set her in the kiddie seat on the front of the cart. He bought puppy chow, a pink glittery collar and leash on a whim, and several chew toys. Halfway to the checkout, he remembered to throw in supplies for himself.

In the truck on the way home, Lizbeth rode on Stony's lap, feet on the window ledge, ears flapping in the wind.

"I reckon even royalty likes ta' feel the wind on their face evry' now and again," laughed Stony.

Lizbeth sniffed every corner of the shanty inside and out while her new master unloaded groceries and rummaged through unpacked boxes for something suitable for a puppy bed. A worn wool Coast Guard blanket left over from Stony's days at sea lined a box of dishes. He unpacked and shook the dust from the blanket before folding it neatly into a thick square and laying it next to the wood stove.

"I'd be honored if you'd keep watch o'er this here keepsake. It kept me warm many a long cold night," said Stony to Lizbeth.

She sniffed the blanket, spun three times and settled, looking to Stony for approval.

"Don't get too rooted. We're goin' out for a ramble. This place needs explorin'."

He fastened the pink collar around her neck and clipped on the leash. "Don't be fussin'. You'll grow out of it soon enough and we'll git ya' somethin' more dignified."

Stony stood outside the door and studied his new property in each direction.

"We might as well start at the top."

He led Lizbeth behind the shanty and found a game trail leading into a forest of Aspen and Ponderosa Pine.

Soon enough, Stony realized the leash was cumbersome and unnecessary. Lined with trees, the trail was too narrow to walk abreast. Lizbeth followed closely behind, only veering off occasionally to sniff at droppings or investigate rustlings in the grass. Stony knelt and unclipped the leash.

"Let's see how you do on your own."

She trotted ahead, thrilled to run free.

Stony was quite a ways down the path before realizing he hadn't heard snuffling in a while. He scanned the trail ahead and panicked when Lizbeth wasn't in sight.

"Lizbeth! Lizbeth!"

Stony hustled down the trail as fast as he could hurry on the narrow uneven surface. He blinked in the sudden sunshine when the dim forest opened into a mountain meadow of native grasses adorned with white, purple, and yellow wildflowers. He stopped short when he saw Lizbeth, her head in a pile of brush off the beaten track.

"Lizbeth. You scared ol' Stony," he said as he swept her up in a relieved hug.

She wiggled and fussed until he set her down, and she ran back to the brush pile.

"What's got yer tail in a twist?" asked Stony.

Expecting a frightened rabbit hiding in a pile of downfall, he was surprised to find numerous cut branches pulled over the top of a hole in the earth. The absence of dirt mounds around the opening told him it wasn't an animal den. On closer inspection, he realized the gap opened into the roof of a dark cavern. A slight breeze flowed through, bringing with it the earthy scent of animals. The puppy continued to whine.

"Shush, Lizbeth. I can't hear a thing with you carryin' on."

In the renewed silence, he leaned close to the hole and listened. A rustling, odd squeaking, and grunts floated through the opening.

"Yep. Some sort of animal down there. Little critters, I reckon."

Stony studied the gap. "Ya' know. I think this is a cave-in from an old mine tunnel."

He scooped Lizbeth into another hug. "Good girl! You found our gold mine. I shoulda' named you Lucky."

Stony studied the landscape and walked the perimeter of the brush heap. On the far side, parallel strips of bent grass and flowers etched a path down the hill and through a makeshift gate in a barbed wire fence.

"I do believe we had a trespasser, Lizbeth. But what in tarnation were they doin' at that hole?"

Dumping garbage? he thought. *And hiding the evidence with branches?*

Down the slope to the west, a ravine split the mountain, north to south.

That looks a likely spot for a mine shaft.

Luring Lizbeth away from the hole proved impossible. The normally obedient puppy began scratching at the rim until Stony was afraid she would fall into the pit. He snapped the leash onto her collar and pulled her along until she reluctantly followed.

Away from the trees and well-used game trail, walking became more difficult. Boulders dotted the ground in irregular patterns, interspersed with gopher holes and prickly pear. Stony carried Lizbeth to protect her delicate paws. Over the ridge, they found another game trail leading into the ravine. At the bottom, dense huckleberry bushes and choke-cherry crowded the path. Stony was thankful he had the foresight to trade in his lightweight boat clothes for sturdy jeans, hiking boots, and a long-sleeved canvas shirt. A misstep had him sliding down the last few feet into a fast-flowing stream previously hidden by the heavy brush. He managed to hold onto Lizbeth and the only damage was to his pride and the seat of his pants. He unclipped the leash and set the squirming puppy on the ground.

"We're out of the rough stuff now. Watch where you step."

Stony stood and surveyed the ravine. Aunt Ida's will mentioned a gold mine connected to the property, but the lawyer said if there was one it had been abandoned long ago. Finding an opening in the overgrowth would be difficult if not impossible. He studied the base of the ravine, searching for the source of the water. A deceivingly small waterfall gushed through a crack in a large boulder.

Whistling to Lizbeth, Stony followed the creek as best he could by listening for the gurgle. Further into the ravine, the brush thinned as did the burbling. He climbed the wall of the ravine and studied the vegetation below. With his new perspective, he could follow a line of thick growth to an area in the far wall.

"That's it, Lizbeth."

Stony traversed the ravine by following the relatively barren rim around to the other side. Looking down from the top, where the growth line met the ravine wall, he could see a decaying wooden frame built into the side of the hill. Faint traces of a once well-worn path led the way to a mine shaft. He glanced to the sinking sun and then the black puppy at his side. "Too late to explore today, Lizbeth, and we don't have the right equipment. No worries. That gold isn't going anywhere. We'll be back someday."

27

"MOST OF THESE missing girls were last seen drinking at Rustler's Roost," said Travis.

"It doesn't surprise me," said Angus. "Just about every lowlife in town can be traced back to that place."

"But other than seeing them at the bar, there aren't any witness statements."

"Nobody saw a thing. That's the typical answer we get when we go in there. *Honor among thieves* and all that."

"So, what can we do?"

"Not much. That many years ago and no witnesses…"

"If girls are going missing at least once a year, don't you think someone knows something?"

"At least one person does, but none of these girls are local. Nobody here knew them, and nobody noticed when they disappeared. The scum who hang out in the Roost aren't going to look sideways at a girl and a guy leaving together."

"Do you think that's how he does it? Gets them drunk and takes them home?"

Angus shrugged. "Makes sense, but the reality is we don't have proof any of them were abducted. They were transient. Maybe they moved on to the next town."

"You don't believe that do you?"

"No, but rule number one—"

"Yeah, yeah, I know. Never assume anything. Work every possibility."

A low murmur of voices outside the window escalated into louder chanting and the thump of boots on the sidewalk below.

"Oh, good grief," said Peter a few moments later from his office.

Angus and Travis stood and peered out the window. A group of picketers were pacing determinedly back and forth in front of the courthouse, holding signs that read 'Bring Our Girls Home' and 'Sheriff Elliott: Resignation or Results.'

Front and center on the courthouse steps were Mavis Vallee and Mayor Kalinski, microphones and cameras in place.

"Any mystery who's behind this one?" asked Peter.

"I don't get it," said Angus "What do those two have against you?"

"I don't think it's personal, either one would rat their grandmother to the press for fifteen minutes of fame."

"What are you going to do about it?"

Peter grabbed his hat and motioned for Zack to stay. "Call their bluff."

Angus grinned and turned to Travis. "We get balcony seats for this show."

They listened as Peter's steps echoed down the hallway, then ran to the window and watched as the door behind Mavis and the mayor flung open. Peter stepped between them and in front of the microphone, effectively stealing the show.

"Everyone, stop," he said in his stern, take-no-prisoners voice. "Stop and listen." He waited for the chanting and pacing to halt. "This office is aware of only one missing woman. She is not from Anderson. She is from Missoula. If any of you have information about any other missing women, please come to the office and file a report. I extend that invitation also to Ms. Vallee and Mayor Kalinski. I repeat. My office is aware of only one missing woman. If any of you have information on other missing women, we welcome you to come to the office and file a report."

Exchanged glances, shrugs, and muttering among the picketers grew louder.

"Hey, Mavis," yelled one irate man. "What gives? You spread the word there were a bunch of women missing from Anderson and the sheriff wasn't investigating."

"Yeah, what gives," yelled a woman. "I got a babysitter so I could come down here for the cause."

"I took time off work," yelled another. "Without pay," she added.

Mayor Kalinski slid behind Mavis and made a run for the door. Peter stepped aside and handed Mavis the microphone, which she promptly dropped and kicked into the lilac bushes, before running through the open door.

"Mavis, stop!" yelled Peter.

Mavis stopped, pasted a 100-watt smile on her face and whirled around.

"Yes, Peter? Did you need something?"

"I need you to stop these ridiculous publicity stunts. You're not helping Stacey Nichols or her family. In fact, you're hurting them. They don't need to hear on the news that the people looking for their daughter are incompetent."

"Why, Peter. We weren't implying anything of the sort."

"Oh, really? 'Resignation or Results?' "

"I didn't make those signs."

"No, but you and our esteemed mayor were the instigators."

"Tell you what, Peter. If you give me priority reporting on any information you find, I'll, ahem, encourage those folks not to picket."

"Mavis, you will be the last person who gets information from my office." He tipped his hat. "Have a wonderful day."

"Well! That's some attitude," said Mavis as Peter stormed up the stairs.

"Angus, go on over to the Roost. We need to question them about that brawl last night. Take Birdie with you if she's up and around."

"Sure, Boss."

"And nobody, I mean NOBODY, says a word to Mavis about anything. We're not going to play her game."

"DOES THIS JOB ever slow down?" asked Birdie with a loud yawn.

"Not while we're in the middle of an investigation," said Angus. "Having second thoughts?"

"Nope."

While Angus tried unsuccessfully to glean information from an uncooperative crowd, Birdie studied the inside of the old building. On a historic level, it was a fascinating old building, with the original timbers and a rough-hewn bar and stools. A woman sitting on the far corner stool watched and when Birdie glanced her way, she beckoned her over with a subtle twitch of her head. Birdie casually made her way in that direction, pretending to study the uniquely carved bar. The woman was as interesting as the bar. Birdie guessed she was in her seventies, but a rough life ages people and she knocked the estimate down a decade. If a hawk could transform into a human, the result was sitting in front of her. Beady dark eyes glittered with the intelligence of a bird of prey.

"Like a drink?" the hawk asked in a gravelly smoker's voice.

"Not on duty," said Birdie, "but I'd take a pop."

Mary motioned to Eddie. "Ice?" she asked Birdie.

"The can is fine."

Drinks delivered, Mary took a sip of hers and a long drag on her cigarette. "You're new in town."

"Birdie Bradshaw." She held out her hand, somewhat repulsed by the arthritis deformed fingers, so like the talons of a bird.

You're letting your imagination run wild. She's just an old barfly.

"Mary. Just Mary." She took another sip of her drink. "Are you helping those folks look for that girl?"

"Yes. Do you know anything that would help?"

"Not with that one, but I know of another."

"Another missing girl?"

"Yeah. It was a long time ago, though, and nobody believed me. They said she ran off with some guy."

A shiver ran down Birdie's spine. She laid her hand on the talon. "Please tell me."

Mary told her about Faith.

"She was a kid. Fifteen at the most. Yeah, she was a runaway, but we took care of her. Gave her the home she never had."

Mary took a long drag on her cigarette and collapsed into a fit of coughing. Recovered, she pinned her sharp gaze on Birdie.

"Something bad happened to her."

"WHAT DID MARY want?" asked Angus when they were back in the car.

"Another story about another missing girl a long time ago."

"How long ago?"

"Forty years, give or take."

"Legitimate?"

"I think so."

⸻◆●◆●◆⸻

THE CHAPEL WAS small, but adequate for the population. Most modern touches had yet to reach Paul's church. Wooden pews, polished to a high shine, were set in even rows, separated by a central aisle. In concession to worldly comforts, the pews were padded and upholstered in a sturdy, but bright cardinal red tweed.

Single arched stained-glass windows decorated the pews, each depicting a different scene from the life and death of Jesus Christ. Sunlight penetrating the colored glass bathed the pews in a warm glow.

Although the building was left unlocked during the day for private worship and Bible studies, for the most part, it remained empty. Buffered from the outside world, the church was Peter's sanctuary. This day he was troubled with feelings of inadequacy. A young woman was missing, possibly dead. Peter was tasked with solving the mystery and the clues were poor.

What am I missing?

A small door set to the side of the sanctuary opened. Paul crossed the platform and stepped into the aisle before he saw Peter, head in hands, in the front pew.

Sitting next to his troubled brother, he said, "I have the honor of being both your brother and pastor. Either way, I'm here to listen."

"Do you think all lawmen have cases that haunt them? Cases they could never solve?" asked Peter, straightening and laying his hands in his lap.

"I think it is probably common." Paul flashed back to the murder of his own parents. Peter's parents. "Are you thinking about Mom and Dad? It's close to the time when... when..." A lump wedged in Paul's throat.

"Yes and no," said Peter. He turned to his brother. "I have the file, you know."

"From their murder?"

"Yes."

"When? How?"

"I've had it for years. It sits next to my chair at home. I haven't had the nerve to look inside. I guess I thought as a sheriff, I could finally solve the case and there would be justice."

Peter and Paul's parents had been robbed and murdered on an anniversary celebration in Missoula when the boys were children. After the murder, they were taken from their home in nearby Princeton and moved to Anderson where they were raised by elderly grandparents. The trauma led Paul into ministry and Peter into law enforcement.

"Peter… the chances of finding whoever did that… so many years ago. There were no witnesses, no evidence."

"No evidence that we know of. We were kids. There might be something in that file—"

"Let it go, Peter. Don't let one evil act define your life."

"I know, Paul. I know I should let go." He shook away those thoughts. "But it's the other case that is bothering me."

"The missing girl?"

"Yeah."

"This case is new, Peter. It's a little early to file it in 'Unsolved Mysteries.' "

"It's been a week. Chances are she's dead and we'll never find the body. Her parents will have to live with that uncertainty for the rest of their lives."

Paul took Peter's hand. "Have faith, Peter. You'll find her."

28

Lizbeth slept on the old wool blanket until Stony fell asleep. She spent the rest of the night cuddled next to him in bed, waking him at sunrise with a lick to his cheek.

"Ugh," Stony said, wiping away the wet. "I'm retired, Lizbeth. There's no need to get up at the crack of dawn."

The puppy jumped from the bed and ran to the door, whining and yipping.

"Ah. Need to relieve yourself. Good girl."

Stony rose, stretched, and crossed the room to open the door. The early mountain air held a crisp chill, but the sun peeked over the mountain, promising a warm summer day.

"I'll fry us up a mess of bacon and eggs, Lizbeth," he called out the door.

How long had he lived by himself on that old boat and never imagined companionship? He thought back on those days and realized the darkness wasn't rain clouds. He was lonely.

Stony fried an extra egg and slice of bacon. He took a tin plate out of his makeshift cupboard and filled it with a scoop of dry puppy chow before mixing in the egg and bacon.

"Here ya go," he said, setting the plate on the floor.

Lizbeth plopped both feet in the middle of the plate, scattering food across the cabin. She ate between her paws until the plate was empty and then wandered the room, eating bits and pieces of scattered food as she found them.

Stony shook his head. "I admire a gal who enjoys her food, Lizbeth."

He cleaned his own plate with much more decorum, then heated water on the stovetop to wash the dishes.

"When I'm finished cleaning up, we'll gather what we need and go explore that mine."

Lizbeth yipped in what Stony chose to believe was agreement.

Behind the shanty leaned a decaying wagon barn. Remnants of red paint hid in the fissures of the dried wood and resolute shingles clung to a rotting roof. Sagging double doors in front were secured with a rusty padlock, but a door on the side of the building stood out in its newness. Stony turned the handle and the door swung open on well-oiled hinges. A layer of dust and grime covered the windows, allowing filtered light into the room. Shiny tools hung in neat rows above a greasy workbench, as out of place as the well-oiled door.

"I wonder what 'ol Ida had going on in here?"

As Stony inspected various clutter in the shed, he was delighted to find his Aunt Ida's hobby was exactly what he needed. A backpack containing several battery-operated miner's headlamps and a box of replacement batteries leaned against the workbench. Next to the pack lay a thick roll of nylon rope and an old lumpy burlap sack.

Stony opened the sack and dumped the contents—several large clods of dirt and rock—onto the workbench. The rocks were covered in the typical red dirt found in the area. As he rubbed the soil away, he found the rocks were actually pieces of quartz. Interspersed in the grain of the quarts were strong veins of shiny gold.

"Gold! Lizbeth! Ida found gold!"

Lizbeth studied Stony with the intensity of a captivated student.

"Where do you suppose she found this?" asked Stony, but he knew. Ida had mentioned the gold mine in her will. It was the lawyer who poo pooed the idea.

Further inspection of the shed found a large blue tarp covering a bulge in the far corner. Stony lifted a corner of the tarp, revealing a small four-wheel ATV. He removed the cover completely. Fastened to the rear of the vehicle were several pickaxes and a small folding garden trolley. A large black plastic crate was fastened behind the driver's seat as a carrier.

"That'll do for you, Lizbeth."

A key hung from the ignition. He turned the key and pressed a button labeled 'start'. The engine roared to life, but soon sputtered and died. The gas gauge needle fluttered at empty. Red plastic containers lined the wall next to the ATV. Stony lifted one and could tell by weight it was full. He unscrewed the cap and sniffed. Gas. A funnel was fitted upside down in the mouth of the container. Stony flipped it around, found and filled the gas tank. The second time around, the motor ignited and continued running.

"The only way to get this thing out of here is through those double doors."

Stony exited through the smaller door and walked around to the front. On closer inspection, he found the rusty padlock on the double doors was unclasped and only turned inward to give the impression of being locked. Unhindered, the doors swung open with surprising ease. He loaded the backpack, rope, and burlap sack into the plastic crate, set Lizbeth on top, and drove the four-wheeler through the wide doorway.

Once outside, he stopped to ponder, recalling the odor and sounds of animals coming from the cave-in. Back in his cabin, he lifted his lever action .30-30 from a hook on the wall, and a box of ammo from a kitchen drawer.

Better to be armed for bear than caught off guard, he thought.

Stony rummaged in a box until he found an old, padded nylon lunch bag. He packed it with jerky, protein bars, and several bottles of water. On his way out, he paused and lifted a padded jacket off a hook by the door.

It'll be cold in that cave.

Outside he stopped to think. The game trail up the mountain was too narrow for the four-wheeler. Unless Aunt Ida knew of another entrance, there had to be a short cut to the mine shaft. He studied the way the mountain rose above the forest and how it sloped to the north. The ravine would be in that direction. His final decision was made when he looked down and found the obvious four-wheeler track leading away from the shed.

"A little extra thinkin' never hurt nobody, Lizbeth." He scratched her behind the ears and climbed onto the driver's seat. "Hang on. Here we go."

The track led to an open area in front of the mine shaft that he was unable to see when climbing through the brush the day before. Any thoughts of driving into the mine were erased when he approached and realized the opening was barely large enough to squeeze through with the garden trolley. Stony found a level area to park and lifted Lizbeth from her seat in the box. She happily ran back and forth, sniffing for rodents while he prepared to explore the mine.

Stony released the bungee cords holding the trolley in place. On the ground, it easily unfolded into a roomy canvas catchall. He emptied the backpack and tested the headlamps before he fitted one on his own head and, imagining the black puppy lost in a dark tunnel, one on Lizbeth. The extra lamp went back in the pack with the box of batteries, a flashlight, and the nylon lunch bag. He dropped the pack into the cart and swung his rifle sling over a shoulder. Chances of running into a bear or mountain lion in the cave midsummer were slim, but he wasn't taking any chances.

Being a sailor, Stony was adept at the tying of all knots. He fastened one end of the rope to a tree growing close to the mine entrance and the other securely to the leather belt around his waist. Not one to take chances, he ensured the clasp on the belt was firmly fastened. This was a day of exploration, so he left the pickaxes and burlap bag on the four-wheeler.

"Come along, Lizbeth," he called to the puppy who was rolling ears over tail trying to remove a burr from her backside.

He eyed the pink leash coiled in the bottom of Lizbeth's carrier box and decided to take his chances. She wasn't inclined to run off and he had his hands full.

Stony grabbed the handle of the trolley, turned on his headlamp and that of Lizbeth and entered the cave. Lizbeth refused to follow. She whined and wiggled and yipped.

"Scared of the boogeyman, Lizbeth?"

Stony backed into the sunlight and lifted Lizbeth into the canvas hold of the trolley where she relaxed, standing on her hind feet with front paws on the rims.

"Try not to squish our lunch."

The headlamps were of high quality and their glow filled the cavern. The solid rock of the walls and ceiling lacked the support beams normally found in a mine tunnel, leading Stony to believe it had begun as a natural cave. Already, the chill permeated his shirt. He stopped to pull on his jacket, lifting the collar against his bare neck.

After gold was discovered, drilling and blasting was used to follow veins of ore. Twin tunnels veered off the main cavern, one to the left and the other to the right, each one supported by heavy timbers. The floor of the cavern was covered with a thick layer of leaves, twigs, and mud, but a definite set of trolley tracks led down the right shaft.

"Let's see what ol' Ida was up to."

He followed the tracks into the right shaft, pulling Lizbeth and the trolley behind him. Blackened blasting and drill marks scarred the tunnel walls, and debris from days gone by lined the edges. Barely a hundred feet in, the tunnel came to an abrupt end. Leaning against the wall was a small pickax, a crowbar, and a sledgehammer. Several burlap sacks were neatly folded in a pile and a large lantern hung from a peg pounded in the wall.

Stony walked over and picked up the ax, impressed that his elderly aunt had the strength to lift such a tool, however the size and weight of the ax was half that of an average tool, as were the crowbar and hammer.

Designed for a child possibly?

At waist level, Stony found the vein, glittering in the light of the lantern.

"There's our retirement fund, Lizbeth." He put a finger to his lips. "Mum's the word."

Reminding himself that today was for exploration rather than prospecting, Stony turned the trolley and followed the tracks back to the main cavern. He entered the remaining shaft, following trolley tracks deep into the mountain. Lizbeth began to whimper and squirm as the tunnel sloped upward, the air freshened, and a faint musky odor followed the breeze. Stony slipped his hand through his rifle sling, ready to shoot at a moment's notice.

Distant murmurs turned to babbles and then, more clearly, the odd rustling and squeaking Stony had heard at the cave-in. He slowed his pace and relaxed his grip on the rifle.

Bats?

Thinking of rabies, he wondered if bats attacked when startled and wished he'd worn a hat.

"Shush, Lizbeth," he whispered. "We don't want to get 'em stirred up."

Ahead, the tunnel curved to the left. Stony stood close to the wall and peered around the bend. He searched the ceiling for black winged rodents, preparing to duck for cover if they took flight. Sunlight filtered through the darkness of the tunnel where a cave-in opened the roof. Several sleeping bats hung upside down from the edges of the roof, undisturbed by his headlamp.

Stony soon realized the squeaking and rustling was coming from lower, toward the floor. A mass of dark squirming bodies formed a lump along the far wall. Several of the creatures shuffled about the chamber. Stony dimmed his light and Lizbeth's. As he watched, he recognized the large round bodies and distinctive quills.

Porcupines? Do they live in caves?

Lizbeth squirmed and whined, trying to jump from the canvas trolley hold.

"No, Lizbeth," said Stony, nudging her deeper into the pack. "Those things will fill you full of quills."

Sensing danger, each porcupine rose, stretched, and left the mound to join the others shuffling deeper into the shaft until nothing was left but a lump of white and pink.

What is that?

Lizbeth, refusing to be contained any longer, crawled out of the pack and scampered to the lump, whining and sniffing. Stony followed.

Oh, no.

Curled in a tight ball, shivering from the sudden loss of her heat source, lay a young blonde woman. Stony knelt next to the girl.

"Miss. Miss." He gently nudged her shoulder with no response.

Stony knew hypothermia. Thirty years in the Coast Guard taught him that. He lifted the rifle from his shoulder and laid it against the tunnel wall. His jacket held the warmth of his body. He took it off and wrapped it around the girl, gently slipping her arms into the sleeves as she shivered and moaned. He was certain she was injured, but not to what extent. Carrying her out was not an option and the small trolley would not hold her. She needed a gurney and medical people and fast. Mostly, she needed to stay alive long enough for that to happen. Stony unlaced his boots, thankful he'd worn long thick woolen socks that morning. He carefully pulled the socks over her bare feet and legs. She was frigidly cold.

"Too cold to make her own heat, Lizbeth."

He studied the puppy. She was by nature a calm dog, even for a puppy.

"Can you stay here and keep her warm?"

Lizbeth yipped.

"I'm not sure if you understand, but let's give it a try."

Stony lifted the puppy and gently laid her against the girl's chest, zipping them both into the padded jacket. Lizbeth's head poked out at the top of the zipper, but she remained quiet.

"Stay, Lizbeth."

Stony turned and ran as fast as he could through the tunnel to the entrance of the cave. The four-wheeler brought him to his house and his truck to the sheriff's office. He stumbled into the courthouse and up the stairs, out of breath and panicked, past Travis at his desk and into Peter's office before he collapsed in a chair.

"Peter! Peter! Help! The girl! In the mine!"

"What girl? What mine?" asked Peter, springing from his chair and rushing to Stony's side.

Travis brought in a cup of water and handed it to the old sailor. He drank too fast, gulped, choked, coughed, and caught his breath.

"The missing girl," said Stony. "I found her in that old mine out at my place."

"Is she alive?" asked Peter.

"She was when I left her, but she won't be for long if we don't get her out of that cold cave."

Peter grabbed his black Search and Rescue cap off a hanger by the door. He looked at Stony.

"Do we need a chopper?"

"We can drive right up to the entrance of the cave faster than calling in a helicopter," said Stony.

"Travis! Call Helen and Angus and whatever EMT is on duty. Tell them to meet me at the Search and Rescue barn."

Travis already had phone in hand. "On it, Boss. Should I call the Nichols?"

Peter hesitated. "No. Let's wait until we get her down the hill. I'd rather know for sure than get their hopes up." Zack whined at his side.

Peter turned to Travis, "Would you drop Zack off at my house on your way home tonight? There's no room for him in the ambulance."

"No worries, Boss. I'll take good care of him."

In the process of gifting his socks to the girl in the cave, Stony's bare feet went back into his boots covered in a layer of mud. Adrenaline made him oblivious to the chafing of wet skin against leather and grit. Off the rush, he was all too aware of painful blisters and sores on his feet. He struggled to keep up with Peter, who waited impatiently while he climbed into the Explorer and buckled his belt.

"Sorry, Peter. My body feels older than its years at the moment."

"No worries, Stony," said Peter, scattering gravel as he roared out of the parking lot. "You help us bring this girl home and you'll be the town hero for the rest of your life. People will be happily waiting on you."

Stone County owned by necessity a sturdy four-wheel drive ambulance capable of traversing many a rugged trail. Peter wore three hats: sheriff, coroner, and head of the county Search and Rescue. On Search and Rescue duty, he insisted on driving the ambulance and easily managed the four-wheeler trail to the mine entrance. Angus and Helen bounced close behind in their Explorer.

Stony led the way into the cave while Helen and Angus hauled a backboard. Peter, the only one who had to stoop through the tunnel, carried blankets, a thermos of warm tea and Helen's CSI kit. EMT Scott Haugen lugged a trauma kit full of medical supplies.

Lizbeth could be heard whining and yipping as they grew closer.

"Hang on, Lizbeth. We're coming," called Stony.

Battered, bruised, and blue, the woman in the mine tunnel was unrecognizable as Stacey Nichols other than the short pink skirt peeking between Stony's thick padded jacket and long wool socks. The crew held their breath as Scott felt for a pulse.

"Weak, but she's alive."

"Thank the Lord," exclaimed Helen.

Stony collapsed in tears of relief and exhaustion. Scott unzipped the padded jacket to free Lizbeth, and she ran to Stony, jumped into his lap and licked his face with enthusiasm.

"You zipped the puppy into her coat for warmth," said Angus. "That's ingenious."

"He probably saved her life," said Scott.

"Lizbeth saved her," said Stony. "Didn't you, Lizbeth. You saved her."

Stony hugged and cuddled his wiggling puppy while the crew wrapped Stacey in a space blanket to hold in what heat she had left and secured her onto the backboard.

"Let's get her out of here," said Scott.

"Are you comfortable staying here alone with your investigation, Helen?" asked Peter.

"Do you have an extra lantern and batteries, Stony?"

Stony rummaged through the pack on the trolley he'd left behind when running for help, pulled out the extra headlamp and box of batteries, and handed them to Helen. He took the lunch bag out of the pack and handed that to her also.

"That'll keep your batteries goin'."

Stony unfastened his headlamp and handed it to Angus.

"You'd best lead the way out, son. I'll hold things up."

Angus nodded and fastened the light strap on his head. He tossed the Explorer keys to Helen.

"I'll ride in the ambulance, Helen. Call if you need anything."

He picked up his end of the backboard as Scott lifted the other end. Peter turned to Stony.

"You next, Stony."

"I'm lame, Peter. Running around with no socks rubbed some nasty blisters into my heels and I'm plain tuckered out. I'll hold things up."

"That's why you're going first, Stony. I want to make sure you don't get left behind. I'm captain of this ship and the captain always goes down last."

"Aye, aye, Captain," said Stony with a salute.

He set Lizbeth in the trolley. Peter took the handle.

"I'll get this, Stony. You concentrate on getting yourself out of here."

Stacey's pulse remained weak but steady as the crew loaded her into the ambulance and started a warming saline IV. Peter helped Stony into the cab of the truck.

"I think we should get you checked out when we get there, Stony. You've had a rough day."

"Naw, Peter. I'm a tough ol' salt."

"At least let them take a look at those blisters."

"I wouldn't mind some relief there," admitted Stony, loosening his boots.

Peter radioed the hospital and then Travis.

"Call the Nichols, Travis. She's alive, but barely."

29

"SHE'S IN SERIOUS condition, but stable," said Dr. Hamm as he and Peter stood outside the one ICU room in Anderson's tiny critical access hospital. "Her parents understandably want to fly her to Missoula. I advised them to let her rest."

"Has she regained consciousness?"

"Only briefly. She knows she's safe from whatever horror she's been through so she's resting easier."

"When will we be able to question her? If whoever did this gets wind she's alive, they'll make a run for it."

"I've sworn all staff to secrecy, but you know how that goes in a small town. Come back tomorrow morning. My guess is she'll be awake and starving."

"I'll bring donuts."

Peter wandered the hospital looking for Stony. He found him in the private doctors' lounge, sprawled out in a plush recliner, a nurse cleaning and bandaging his damaged feet.

"What's the verdict, Nurse?"

She smiled and fastened the final wrap. "Disinfected and bandaged. If he promises to keep them clean and dry, and wear socks, he'll probably make it."

"Good news. Thanks."

The nurse gathered her things and left the room. Peter sat in an equally plush chair next to Stony.

"I would say we're in the wrong profession."

"I may get a blister now and then, so I have an excuse to hang out in the doctors' lounge," laughed Stony. "Speaking of verdicts, how's our girl?"

"Downgraded from critical to serious, but stable. They expect she'll be sitting up for a big breakfast tomorrow."

"Is she in as bad a shape as we thought?"

"Pretty much. Now that all the excitement is over, how exactly did you find her?"

"I had a few days free so thought I'd explore the property. Lizbeth—"

"The puppy?"

"Yeah. Lizbeth and I followed a path through the trees yesterday and she found that cave-in. I didn't think anything of it. I figured some rascal was dumping garbage in the hole instead of hauling it all the way to the landfill."

"Where did you get the puppy?"

"Oh, I went into town yesterday for supplies and a kid had a box full of those wigglers in front of the grocery store. He was donatin' them to worthy homes."

"I'd guess you got the pick of the litter."

"You would guess correctly. Of course, I didn't know at the time how useful she'd be."

"So, what happened today?"

"I git the feeling this is an interrogation."

"Not subtle enough?"

"You could use some work on your technique."

"Sorry, Stony, but it has to be done."

"No worries, Sheriff. Ask me anything you want."

"Tell me about today."

"Lizbeth was up at the crack of dawn. Let's hope she grows out of that one. Do you know she expected to spend the night cuddled up in bed with me?!"

"Women." Eye roll.

"Anyway, she was up at the crack of dawn, so I made us bacon and eggs and mixed some with puppy chow for Lizbeth. She seemed to enjoy that."

"We could skip to the details pertinent to the investigation."

Stony's eyes twinkled. "Five syllables, Sheriff. You law men and your fancy talk."

"I expect you're more educated than you let on, Stony."

Stony laughed. "Maybe so, Sheriff. Maybe so. Anyhoo, with much ado and crawling through brush and bramble, Lizbeth and I found the entrance to the mine yesterday. This morning we happened upon the four-wheeler, headlamps, and such in an old shed behind the shanty. Following the four-wheeler track from the shed to the mine entrance proved to be a much more desirable route."

"I'll bet."

"The mine has two tunnels as you probably noticed. We explored the one on the right first. It's a dead end. Then we went down the second one, where we found the girl. She was moanin' and stirrin' enough I knew she was alive so I bundled her up as best I could and zipped Lizbeth in next to her to keep her warm and ran for help."

"You had no idea she was there?"

"If'n I had, I woulda' rescued her sooner."

"What were you expecting to find down there?"

"Gold, Sheriff. It is a gold mine."

"Put your shoes on and I'll give you a ride home."

⬥

PETER AND THE crew gathered in his office.

"Hypothermia was her immediate issue. She's been beaten several times. Broken ribs and a wrist possibly from earlier. The broken ankle is fresher, possibly from the fall. No sign of rape."

"So, she was pushed through the cave-in?" asked Angus.

"No doubt," said Helen. "The tire tracks leading to the opening were the first clue. I found signs of a struggle and strands of pink thread where her skirt caught on branches."

"Anything else?" asked Peter.

"I made casts of the tire tracks and followed them down the hill. They met up with a well-traveled county road, you know, that one that goes to Bear Lake. There was no way to follow the trail."

"So, it could have been anyone."

"Travis is working on the tire casts. He can use the Tread Design Guide and narrow them down to a specific tire and type of vehicle. I know the number one rule is not to assume anything, but I think we can start by assuming this is someone local."

"I agree," said Peter. "That cave-in is pretty isolated. I doubt an outsider would know about it."

"What about Stony?" asked Birdie, still smarting from being the only deputy not included in the rescue. "Isn't the mine on his land?"

"It is, yes, but the tire tracks go through the fence. Someone cut the barbed wire and fashioned a makeshift gate. Afterwards they pulled it shut, undetectable unless someone, like me, looks at it closely," said Helen.

"We can't assume that Stony is innocent at any rate," said Peter. "I questioned him earlier today, Birdie, but we need to look into his whereabouts and alibi from when Stacey went missing until she was rescued. Could you take care of that?"

"Yes, sir," said Birdie, appeased.

"There's something else," said Helen, swallowing hard. "Down in that tunnel... there were bones. Lots of bones. Human bones." Her eyes teared. "Stacey Nichols wasn't the first. She's the only one who survived."

"Selina," whispered Birdie.

"How far did you get on documenting everything?" asked Peter.

"Barely touched the surface. I need lights, boxes for the bones, and help. And it's cold down there. I wouldn't say no to a space heater."

"Any problems with the porcupines?"

"No. It's odd. They seem comfortable around me, like they're used to being around humans."

"That could explain why they cuddled up to Stacey. Doc says she wouldn't have survived as long as she did without their body heat."

"I'll get the generators, lights, and heaters out of the Search and Rescue barn," offered Angus.

"Thanks, Angus. If you would haul them to the site and get them set up that would be great."

"On it," said Angus on his way out the door.

"Helen, call Clem to help with documentation. Besides you, she's our best forensics person and she'll be thrilled to work a real case. Birdie, you go with Helen. Travis can help document when you get things back here."

"Thanks, Peter," said Helen on her way out.

Birdie hesitated. "Sheriff. I need to talk to you about something."

"Sure, Birdie," he said, curious at her formality and sensing an impending confession. "What's going on?"

She told Peter about her missing friend Selina and subsequent application to the criminal justice program at community college. "That weekend Selina disappeared was the best thing that ever happened to me," said Birdie, then clapped a hand to her mouth. "That didn't come out right. I mean, if Selina hadn't gone missing, I would probably still be working at that clothing store to support my weekend partying. Instead, I found my true calling."

"Good enough," said Peter, thinking of the case file sitting beside his easy chair at home. "Thank you for letting me know. That explains the mystery of you wanting to work in Anderson."

Birdie turned to go.

"Birdie, hold on," said Peter.

She stopped and turned. "Yes?"

"You know we may never know if any of those bones belong to your friend Selina."

"I know, Peter, but if we find who's doing this…"

30

IN SPITE OF the early hour, Mavis and Mayor Kalinski, flanked by KRUD TV, were holding court in front of the hospital. Peter drove past and parked behind the ER entrance. He wasn't interested in whatever narrative they were pushing.

Stacey had been moved out of ICU into a regular patient room. Her parents were at her side but jumped up at Peter's entrance. Karyn gave him a bear hug and Jarod shook his hand.

"This is Sheriff Elliott, Stacey," said Karyn. "He's been searching for you since you disappeared. His department brought you out of that mine yesterday."

Stacey set her fork on the breakfast tray and held out her hand.

"Thank you so much, Sheriff. I... the doctor told me I wouldn't have survived much longer."

"Later, I'll introduce you to the man who found you. His quick thinking kept you warm until we got there."

"They mentioned something about porcupines and a puppy," said a confused Jarod, "but we didn't get the details."

"For some reason, the porcupines in that cave are comfortable around humans. They may have been attracted to Stacey's warmth."

"They were licking me," said Stacey. "I remember the licking, but it didn't scare me because of Ben."

"Ben?" asked Peter.

Stacey looked confused for a moment and shook her head to clear the cobwebs.

"Yeah. There was an old guy named Ben." She turned to her mother. "He reminded me of Grandpa."

"Was he the one who kidnapped you?" asked Peter.

"No... yes... maybe." Stacey put both hands to her head and rubbed her temples.

"Really, Sheriff," said Karyn, taking Stacey's hand and beaming at her daughter. "Is this necessary? Stacey is alive and safe. That's all that matters."

Peter met Jarod's eyes. "Can I speak with you outside?"

"Sure, Sheriff." He patted Stacey on the shoulder. "I'll be right back, sweetie."

Stacey recoiled. "Don't call me that!"

"Um… okay."

Jarod frowned and followed Peter out the door.

"I've been calling her sweetie since she was born."

Peter shrugged. "She's on a lot of medications, but it might have something to do with the kidnapping."

"Whoever did this to her… I want them found."

"I agree. I need your help. Any information you can get out of Stacey, I need you to share with me as soon as possible. Names, locations… anything."

"Will do, Sheriff."

"Thanks. Now I have to find an old guy named Ben."

Peter hurried down the hall. Out in his Explorer, he called the office.

"Travis, I want anyone available on the crew to ask around about an old guy named Ben. Tell them to be discreet."

"Is this about Stacey Nichols?"

"Yep."

THE MOST DISCREET person in the most discreet place in town was Mary at Rustler's Roost, at least in Angus's mind, and that is where he went. Mary sat on her usual stool at the far end of the bar, filling out a supply order and nursing the dregs of an amber liquid that Angus pegged as whiskey. He pulled the next stool closer.

"Buy you a drink?"

"It's been a decade or two since I've had an offer like that from a good-lookin' young buck. Let me pretend for a minute you're not a deputy looking for information."

Angus grinned. "For good information I'll buy you a double."

"Deal." She peered at him over her half-moon reading glasses. "You understand, of course, certain information is off limits."

"As always."

Angus motioned to Eddie, the bartender, who poured Mary a double shot of her favorite whiskey.

"You're sure of yourself," said Mary.

"We found the missing girl. Now we need to find the person who took her."

"You talked to the new deputy… the pretty dark-haired girl."

"Birdie. She told me about your friend who went missing."

"It was years ago."

"Not so long ago it couldn't be the same person."

"What do you know?"

"We have a tip that an old guy named Ben was involved. Would've been a young guy named Ben all those years ago."

Mary sipped her whiskey and lit a cigarette and thought of all the men who she'd known through the years... all the men who were now old and still sitting on the same old barstools, drinking and smoking and telling the same old stories.

"I don't think I've known someone named Ben in my entire life," she said.

"Think hard, Mary. This could save lives."

"Really, Angus. I've been here since I was what, fifteen? I couldn't tell you the ones passing through, but the locals, I know every one of them."

"No Bens?"

"No Bens."

"Benjamin?"

Mary rolled her eyes. "No Benjamins."

Angus sighed and drummed his fingers on the bar. "Okay. Thanks, Mary. Let us know if anything comes to mind."

⸺●◦●◦●◦●⸺

PETER TURNED TO the most discreet people he knew in town, his brother Paul and the Pastors Association.

"I can't think of any Bens," said Paul. "It's not a common name in this area."

Paul removed a list of numbers tacked to the bulletin board over his office desk.

"Phone numbers for Pastors Association members," he explained.

A half-dozen calls and an hour later, they were no closer to finding an old man named Ben.

"One third grader and a ninety-year-old with dementia in the nursing home," said Paul. "If this Ben is local, he's not on the church radar."

Linda came into the room and Peter explained the situation.

"I can't think of any Bens either. I help out at the senior center once a week. There aren't any Bens active in that group."

"Okay, thanks. Let me know if you think of anyone."

Travis didn't know any discreet people, but he knew someone who knew everyone, Mabel Morse, at the Chamber of Commerce.

"Hi Mabel, this is Travis over at the sheriff's office."

"You're not going to make me lift any heavy books, are you? I spent the evening sitting on a hot water bottle after your last call."

"Uh… no… I mean I don't think so. I wanted to ask you if you knew someone."

"I know plenty of people, but if you're looking for gossip, you've called the right place." Raucous laughter ended in a coughing fit and then silence.

"Mabel? Mabel? Are you all right?"

"Gasp… yeah, I laughed so hard I lost my breath. I may have wet my pants, too, but I'll take care of that later. Now, who did you want dirt on?"

Ignoring the mental image, Travis asked, "Do you know anyone by the name of Ben?"

"Just Ben? No last name?"

"All I know is the first name."

"Is this part of an investigation?" whispered Mabel.

"Yes," whispered Travis back, "but I can't tell you any details."

"Dang. Well, let me think."

Crickets.

"Mabel?"

"I'm thinking. Be patient."

Crickets

"Nope, not anyone living anyway. Do they have to be alive?"

"Yes, Mabel. It is a recent crime. Let me know if you think of anyone."

⋯⋯•◆•⋯⋯

PETER TOOK A chance and drove back to the hospital. Mavis and the mayor had long since abandoned their press conference, so he entered through the front door. A receptionist stopped him in his tracks with a smirk.

"The Nichols family has requested no visitors… 'especially Sheriff Elliott' were the words of Mrs. Nichols."

Peter studied the smirk. The young ones aged, but maturity wasn't guaranteed. This one reminded him of a frequent flyer through the community service program for minors caught with alcohol. She had a chip on her shoulder and delighted in her momentary power over the sheriff who sent her there.

"Sheila, isn't it?"

The smirk drooped. "Uh… yeah."

Peter smiled. "It's nice to see you working to pay off all those fines. I know it was a strain on your parents."

Sheila reddened and dropped her eyes to her computer screen. Peter chastised himself for the snide remark.

"Sheila?"

Two brown eyes brimming with tears met his.

"You're doing great, I'm proud of you."

31

IN MOST SITUATIONS, bringing light on a subject is a positive. Illuminating the mine shaft where Stacey Nichols was found turned the cover of darkness into a cave of horrors.

"At least they didn't all die in the same spot," said Helen. "Cataloging bones will be easier."

Below the cave-in, the largest pile of bones consisted of those too injured to move, dead when they hit the floor, or they never regained consciousness. Intermixed among the bones were fragments of fabric. Blue nylon shorts, multicolored spandex leggings. Single skeletons gathered at the edges of the cave walls. Those were the not so lucky victims, the ones who died slowly, aware they had no hope.

"Natural fibers like cotton and linen decompose faster," said Clem. "We won't see much of that."

Birdie stifled a scream. A rubber soled sandal lay at the edge of the pile, foot bones and several toes firmly fastened in leather straps. *Get used to it, Birdie. This is your life now.*

"How many bodies do you think are down here?" she asked.

Helen counted visible skulls. "Thirty or forty? There seem to be more skulls than other bones."

"Probably carried off by predators," said Birdie.

"Or eaten by the porcupines," said Clem. "That's the problem with porcupines. Bones are full of minerals that they need in their diet. They eat the evidence."

Birdie gasped. "This is a giant porcupine buffet. That's why they're here. Did they eat the bodies, too?"

"No. Only the bones after the bodies decayed. Porcupines are vegetarians."

Blocking the thought of porcupines gnawing at her bones, Birdie said, "Where do we start?"

Helen, most adept at processing crime scenes, took the lead. She handed Birdie a set of pre-numbered plastic evidence cards and a digital camera.

"Glove up and start over there."

She pointed to the far end of the cave.

"Pick a skeleton to be number one, place the card next to it and take as many photographs as you think we need from every angle. You can't overdo digital photography. When you're finished with number one, let Clem know and move on to number two."

Helen handed Clem a box of evidence tags and a logbook. She pointed to a stack of evidence boxes. "When Birdie is finished with a skeleton, find the box with the corresponding number and start the process of tagging and logging the bones. Leave the place marked so we can come back and sift for more evidence if needed."

Helen sighed. "And I'll work on this pile in the middle."

Birdie was on her fifth skeleton when she found the necklace wrapped around remnants of ribs. She dropped to her knees, tears clouding her vision. A thick layer of dust covered the deep brown crystal. Birdie had no doubt it was the necklace Selina never removed, even in death. Selina said something about the crystal releasing negative energy. Birdie cynically wondered if a crystal meant for protection would have been a better choice.

32

R EGULARS GATHERED IN the late afternoons at Rustler's Roost. Most came to play darts or pool. A few sat and drank and watched, choosing to be on the fringes of the group rather than home entirely alone. Mary ignored the women, but studied the men, reciting their names in her head as she swept the room.

The dart players. Joe, Marty, Butch, Larry. Allen on the sidelines. His regular partner… *oh, yeah, Georgie.* Georgie had been missing lately, his wife had cancer and he was spending evenings home with her. *Sad,* thought Mary. *His wife had to be terminally ill to get his attention.*

The pool shooters. Bob, another Joe, Steve, and Danny at one table. Wayne, Mike, Bill, and Hank at the other.

The hangers-on. Old Frank sitting at the table across from Allen. A stroke knocked him out of the dart league, but he could still hold a beer bottle. His wife dropped him off every afternoon. *I suppose it's better than a babysitter.*

Ebenezer sat in his usual place in the far corner table. A cold chill brushed the back of Mary's neck. The guy gave her the creeps. When she was younger, he would try and get her to go home with him. She never had a reason, good or bad.

Ebenezer. Eb... en... BEN... Could it be?

Mary jumped off her stool and ran into the office, yanking her jacket off the coat tree in the corner, tipping it onto the floor.

Eddie ran into the office. "Are you okay?"

"Yeah, fine," she said, setting the tree upright. "I need to go out for a bit. Can you handle things on your own?"

"Sure. Everything okay?"

"Yeah, yeah. I need to run an errand."

⁕

FOOTSTEPS RUSHING UP the stairs and down the hall to the sheriff's office had become routine enough that Travis didn't look up until two hands slapped the top of his desk.

"I need to talk to Angus," said a breathless Mary.

"He's out on a call. Could someone else help you?"

"The girl?"

"Everyone is out except the sheriff."

"What can I help you with, Mary?" asked Peter, coming out of his office.

"I know who Ben is."

"Ben? The Nichols kidnapper?"

"Yes. I mean, I think so."

"Bring us in some tea, would you, Travis?'

Peter led Mary into his office and had her sit in a soft leather chair in front of his desk.

"Tell me what you know, Mary."

"Angus came in asking me if I knew anyone named Ben. He said it might be the name of the kidnapper. I couldn't think of anyone at the time, but then today I was watching all the regulars."

Travis handed her a cup of tea and she took a sip.

"There's a whole lot of Steves and Joes and Bobs, but no Bens. Then I saw him sitting there and I knew. I knew it was him."

"Who Mary?"

"There's a creepy old guy named Ebenezer. He's been coming in for as long as I've been around. He used to try and get me to go home with him, but he makes my skin crawl. You know?"

"Sure, Mary. How are you connecting this with the kidnapper?"

"Ebenezer. E. BEN. Ezer. See. Like a Thomas goes by Tom or Jonathan goes by John."

"Kind of a long shot, but I can check it out. You say he's at the Roost now?"

"He was when I left."

Peter followed Mary out and into the parking lot.

"I'll meet you there, Mary, and you can point this guy out."

Mary and Peter walked into Rustler's Roost together. Peter followed her to the far corner where she collapsed into a booth and put her head in her hands.

"He's gone. He's going to get away."

"Is there any reason he would know you were coming to the sheriff's office?"

"Well, no."

"Then he went home. Do you know where he lives?"

"I don't even know his last name, Peter. I stay as far away from him as I can."

Not normally inclined to cooperate with law enforcement, the regulars made an exception as a favor to Mary.

"Do any of you know the man named Ebenezer who was sitting in the corner booth earlier?" asked Peter.

He was answered with a room full of shaking heads.

"He's in here on a regular basis and nobody knows him?"

"It's not that we don't know who he is, Sheriff. It's that we don't know anything about him," explained a grizzly man covered in black leather and tattoos. "He sits over there by himself and doesn't talk to anyone."

"I know him," said a quavering voice.

"That's Old Frank," said Mary. "He's about the oldest person here."

Allen moved so Peter could sit across from Frank. "What do you know about him?"

"He's a bit younger than me, but we both went to school here in Anderson. He had a rough time of it if I remember right. I don't know anything about his parents, but he reeked of neglect. Clothes never fit. No lunch money. That kind of thing. Of course, that meant he was bullied. Always kinda felt sorry for him."

"Do you know where he lives?"

"East of town. My folks called it the Hatcher place. I guess that was his family name."

33

ENEZER HAD NEVER had a friend. Males and females alike mocked him at worst and ignored him at best. For a few years, after graduating high school, Ebenezer worked as a night stocker in the local grocery store. Social interaction was minimal, which suited him. No contact meant no bullying and he'd had enough of that to last him a lifetime. One mid-November evening, he arrived at work to find a new employee opening shipping boxes in the holiday aisle. He stood for a moment, dismayed at the invasion of his quiet space.

"Hi," said the pretty girl, tossing her wavy blonde hair. "You must be Ebenezer."

"Uh, yeah."

"I'm Becky."

"So, you, uh, work here now?"

"Yeah. Temporary holiday help, but they said it could work into full time if I do a good job."

And that's how it began, Becky chattering on into the night about her friends and hair and clothes and other subjects Ebenezer found uninteresting. Since she didn't expect him to participate in the conversation, he didn't feel the pressure of most social situations and grew accustomed to the babble.

One night, as Ebenezer made his way down an aisle, a box of pasta fell at his feet.

"Oops! I'm sorry," said Becky, from a ladder above. "It slipped out of my hand."

Ebenezer stooped, retrieved the box, and handed it to Becky.

"Thanks, Ebenezer," she said, flashing a smile.

Later that night, Ebenezer realized the chatter had stopped. He looked up from his work and found Becky staring at him with unusual interest.

"I really enjoy working with you, Ebenezer," she said.

"Uh... okay."

"I'm always yakking away. My mom says I talk too much. You know all kinds of things about me, and I don't know anything about you."

"Uh... I guess so."

"We should get together after work. You know, go have a soda pop or something."

Ebenezer felt panic rising. He clenched his fists and willed himself not to run. People showing interest never ended well for him. He preferred to remain invisible.

"I… uh… go home after work," he said, deflecting the invitation.

"Sure, Ebenezer. I understand."

The next night, Becky met him at work with two bottles of Pepsi-Cola and a white bakery bag filled with danish.

"We can have our soda here before work," she said, handing him a bottle.

Ebenezer had never had a soda and wasn't sure what to expect, but he took the bottle and tried a swig. It was sweet, but good, and the bubbles tickled his nose. He smiled a rare smile and reached into the offered bakery bag. He couldn't say he had a favorite danish. Sweet treats were not a big part of his childhood, but the ones Becky brought were delicious.

Every night after that, Becky would bring a different flavored soda and a bag of treats. Instead of endless chatter about herself, she would ask Ebenezer questions. His answers at first were short and vague. As days and weeks passed, wariness faded into the background, replaced with acceptance, and then trust. Ebenezer had his first friend. He deflected the most personal questions. He didn't want this pretty girl to hear about his abusive parents and the bullying at school.

Ebenezer, inexperienced with social cues, missed the subtle changes. Becky was patient. She didn't want to scare him away. Every night she would sit a little closer, millimeters really. Eventually they relaxed side by side, laughing about weird food choices, "who eats pickled pigs feet?" and other oddities of life. For the first time, Ebenezer felt normal.

"Ebenezer?"

"Yeah, Becky?"

"Do you ever think about getting married?"

"Naw. I don't think anyone would marry me."

"What about me?"

"You're great, Becky. I bet plenty of guys would want to marry you."

"No, silly, I mean you. Do you ever think about marrying me?"

Ebenezer blushed. "Naw. I wouldn't ever think you would want to marry me."

"I do though, Ebenezer. I do want to marry you."

Shocked into silence, Ebenezer stared with his mouth half-mast.

Becky laughed and gave him a hug. "Let's do it, Ebenezer. Let's get married."

"Uh… okay."

Contemplations of odd food items were replaced with talk of wedding dresses and honeymoon locations. Ebenezer wandered in a dream state, unable to completely grasp the wonderful thing that was happening. He willingly left all planning to Becky, happily contributing to expenses whenever she asked.

Ebenezer's mother wasn't thrilled about the wedding plans. She's the one who suffered through nine months of pregnancy. She was the one who had to change his miserable diapers and keep him fed until he could take care of himself. She deserved his undivided loyalty and devotion. How could he take care of her if he was taking care of a wife? She watched as Ebenezer slipped the rented tuxedo out of its garment bag.

"Please, Mama. Please come to my wedding. I told Becky you would be there."

Mama took a long drag on her cigarette, flicking the ash toward Ebenezer.

"What kind of girl would want to marry a worthless piece of garbage like you?"

"She doesn't think I'm garbage. She loves me."

Months of harassment and hate couldn't dampen Ebenezer's bliss. There was only one option left.

"All right, I'll go to your stupid wedding."

"What?!" Ebenezer hadn't been so surprised since Becky asked him to get married.

"I said I'll go to your stupid wedding. Are ya' deaf?"

Ebenezer ran to his bedroom and came out with another garment bag.

"I bought you a new dress, Mama. You'll be the prettiest one there besides Becky."

The mean-hearted woman had a fleeting twinge of regret when she saw the exquisite dress, delicate chiffon the color of bluebells. She thought of a day long ago when she had married for love.

"I worked an extra weekend to buy that for you, Mama."

She shook herself back into reality. Nope. The wedding must be stopped if she had to go there and do it herself.

While Ebenezer drove his mother to the little white church at the edge of town, his mother plotted her destruction and Ebenezer dreamt about his wedding. Becky had described everything in such minute detail that he could see it in his mind, the pews covered in baby pink and white roses, his beautiful bride standing on the steps of the church, eagerly awaiting his arrival.

"What time is it, Mama?" asked Ebenezer, as they pulled into the church parking lot.

"How would I know? I don't own no fancy pants watch."

He looked around in bewilderment. Where were all the guests Becky bragged about? All her family and friends?

"Maybe everyone walked over from Becky's house," said Ebenezer.

"Yeah, whatever. Let's get this thing over with."

Ebenezer took his mama's arm like he'd been practicing. He was proud of the dress he picked out for his mother. It brought out a hint of the beauty she had once been. He made a handsome groom in his rented tux if he did say so himself. He imagined the reaction as they walked into the church full of well-wishers.

Ebenezer gave his mother's arm a squeeze. "Here we go." And he opened the door to the empty church.

A neighbor, watching through a window across the street, saw the young man and older woman enter the church and then walk out, standing on the steps looking around in bewilderment. She called out to them from her doorway.

"Excuse me. Are you looking for someone?"

"Becky," said Ebenezer. "I'm looking for Becky. There's supposed to be a wedding today."

"Becky Pierson?"

"Um, yeah."

"I'm sorry, honey. You're at the right place and time, but the wrong day. Becky got married yesterday to that nice Benson boy. Are you friends of the family?"

Ebenezer's mama laughed until she couldn't breathe. She fell to the ground and gasped until she turned blue. Ebenezer's mama and his soul both died that day.

34

"I HAVE AN ADDRESS," said Travis. "He's down the road from the cave-in where you found Stacey, so it makes sense."

"Call Angus and Tom. Brief them on the situation and have them meet me at the entrance to Ebenezer's property. I don't want to go in without backup."

"Are you sure this is the right guy?"

"No, but, if it is, we need to be prepared."

Visitors were rare so Ben was startled to hear tires crunching gravel outside his cabin door, even more so when he looked out the window and saw three Stone County sheriff vehicles. He opened the door and waved to the officers.

"Can I help you folks?"

Sensing no danger, Peter motioned for Angus and Tom to stay in their vehicles rather than escalate the situation with a three-officer confrontation. Peter raised his hand in a friendly gesture as he approached.

"We're looking for a man named Ebenezer."

"No. No," said Ben. "My name's Ben."

"Good to meet you, Ben. Peter Elliott, Stone County sheriff," said Peter, taking the hand Ben offered in greeting.

Peter noted Ben's hand during the shake. Strong, callused, and dry, free of the shaking or sweating he often found in nervous and guilty people.

"Do you mind if my deputies and I come in and ask a few questions?"

"Come on in," said Ben, motioning to the other men. "I'll put on the coffee pot. It's not often I get company up here on the mountain."

Angus and Tom exited their vehicles and followed Peter into the small cabin. Ben busied himself at the cookstove, throwing logs in the fire and filling an old-fashioned percolator with water from a spigot.

"There's a couple extra folding chairs along the wall," said Ben, motioning toward a single bed set up on the far side of the room.

Peter scanned the room on his way to gather chairs. The cabin was rustic, but clean, which made it easier to spot the blue nylon rope hanging from the bed frame. On the way back, he studied the rough plank floor. A rusty brown smear stained the wood in his path. He followed the smear to a large blotch next to the bed. Blood.

Ben poured boiled coffee into large tin mugs, chatting with the enthusiasm of a lonely person enjoying unexpected visitors.

"Sit down. Sit down," said Ben to Angus and Tom, setting filled mugs on the table next to the two kitchen chairs.

He helped Peter unfold the other chairs and handed him a mug.

"I bought treats in town yesterday," he said, placing a white bakery bag of donuts on the table.

"Thanks, Ben," said Peter, taking a donut, but ignoring the coffee. "Do you live here by yourself?"

Ben hesitated. "In this cabin? Yep. Yep. By myself."

"Have you lived here long?"

"Ever since Mama died. Her house is up the hill. I like having my own place."

"Have you always lived here alone?"

Confusion crossed Ben's face. "Yeah. Alone."

"Do you ever have company? Overnight company?"

"Uh… sometimes." He put his hands to his temples. "Ebenezer."

"Who is Ebenezer, Ben?"

"He lives up the hill. In Mama's house." Ben jumped up, knocking his chair over. "You should go. Ebenezer will be angry if he finds you here."

Tom stood, set Ben's chair upright and leaned against the door.

"Sit down, Ben. Tell us about Ebenezer," said Peter.

Ben's eyes rolled in terror. His hands shook and his voice trembled as he spoke.

"You don't want to make Ebenezer angry." His voice fell to a whisper. "He hurts people."

"Has he hurt you, Ben?"

Again confusion. "Uh… no, but he hurts them." His eyes strayed to the bed.

"Who does he hurt, Ben?"

Tears formed in Ben's eyes. "The girls. He hurts the girls."

Peter stood and walked over to the bed. "I noticed this rope fastened to the bedframe. Can you tell me about this?"

"Ebenezer. He brought them here. I tried to take care of them. He hurt them."

Peter pointed to the stains on the floor. "This looks like dried blood, Ben."

"She was hurt. I brought her bandages and medicine."

Peter remembered the old man in the pharmacy, the one trying to buy bandages and the rude pharmacist.

"Is Ebenezer home now?"

"Uh… I don't know."

"Ben, I'd like you to come into town with us. You can tell us more about Ebenezer and the girls."

"I can't make him angry."

"Ebenezer can't hurt you if you come with us."

Peter helped the trembling Ben to his feet and led him out the door. "How do we get to Ebenezer's place, Ben?"

Ben pointed to the two-lane track leading around his cabin and up the hill.

"You guys go check it out. I'll bring Ben into town."

"Sure, Boss," said Tom.

"Shouldn't you cuff him?" mouthed Angus.

Peter shook his head. Ben showed no signs of violence, and he would be secured in the back of the vehicle. Peter questioned that decision as he helped Ben into the back seat of his Explorer and heard a low menacing growl coming from Zack in the adjacent container.

"Dogs don't like me," said Ben.

And Zack is never wrong, thought Peter.

<hr>

TOM AND ANGUS found a ramshackle log cabin at the end of the trail. Unchecked pine seedlings in different stages of growth surrounded the side walls while chokecherry trees grew to the height of the roof on each front corner. A lilac bush stood guard by the front door, daring anyone to enter.

"It looks abandoned," said Tom through his open window as he and Angus parked side by side in front of the house.

"If someone lives here, they go through a back door. The weeds growing on that path haven't been disturbed for a while," said Angus.

"Let's check it out."

Angus walked around the back of the cabin while Tom knocked on the front door. The house was a typical old homestead that started as a one-room cabin, with more rooms added as the family grew and funds and supplies were available. Besides the original log structure, there was a wide back room built with rough-sawn lumber opening out onto a covered porch. On the far side, another room of sawmill cut boards gave the cabin the look of a modern home. Angus knocked on the back door and announced himself before he tried the knob. Unlocked. He circled back around to the front.

"Find anything?" asked Tom.

"Looks neglected back there, too. Nobody's using the back door, but it's unlocked."

"This one too. Can we call it an abandoned shack and take a look?"

"Sounds okay to me. If this Ebenezer is in there, he's long past needing help."

Tom stood on the toes of his boots and peered through a small window in the upper panel of the door before turning the knob.

"Ebenezer. Stone County Sheriff's Department," he said, as he stepped in the doorway.

No answer.

Angus and Tom entered a long-ago deserted room. Windows on each side of the front door and one in each of the outer walls let in sufficient light. Dust danced in the sunlight and piled in layers along every surface. Cobwebs swayed in long strands from ceiling and doorways.

"I don't think anyone lives here," said Angus.

"Nope." Tom walked over to a kitchen table set under the window and swiped a finger along the surface. "Look at this," he said, holding up his clean finger to Angus.

Angus walked over and studied the table. "No dust. Weird."

He turned and scanned the rest of the room. A mismatched set of rocking chairs faced a wood burning stove in the opposite corner. The smaller, daintier chair was covered in dust. A side table stood between the chairs. The table itself was covered in a layer of grime, but a book lying on the table looked recently read. Angus reached out to pick up the book.

"Stop!" said Tom. "Put gloves on first. Who knows, this may be a crime scene. Something weird is going on here."

"You're right." Angus pulled a pair of nitrile gloves out of his pocket, although he left the book on the table. "It's a romance novel. My mom was reading that same one last time I was home."

"Fairly recent then?"

"Yep. Mom reads them so fast; she's always waiting for the new ones to come out."

"Weird... I mean about the book here, not your mom."

Angus laughed. "I never did get into romance novels myself."

"That chair has been sat in recently, too," said Tom, examining the larger of the rocking chairs. No dust."

Angus opened the stove's firebox. A partially burned log lay in a pile of ash. "That wood is fresh, too."

He turned and walked through a doorway leading to the back of the house. Dingy yellow metal cabinets circa 1950s filled the narrow space. A faint odor of cooking oil hung in the air.

"Is there electricity up here?" asked Tom.

"Must be. I didn't notice a propane tank when I did my walk-around."

Angus opened the refrigerator door. "Something's keeping this going."

A lone jar of pickles and a dried-out hunk of cheese sat on the top shelf. A half jar of mustard stood in the door. The freezer department contained several packages wrapped in butcher paper.

"Home butchered meat?" asked Tom.

"Could be anything. Lots of folks around here butcher their own wild meat or buy beef from ranchers."

Tom found a dirty cast iron frying pan on the stove top. A plate and utensils sat unwashed in the sink. The cupboards were covered in layers of grime.

"This is so strange," he said. "Do you suppose a lost hiker came in here and stayed the night?"

"And brought pickles and cheese and meat and read a romance novel?"

Tom shrugged. They left the kitchen and walked through the living room and into the other addition. An antique cast iron bed frame with an ivory finish filled most of the room. The bed had been slept in and left unmade.

Angus opened the top drawer of a mirrored pine dresser pushed against the back wall. It contained an assortment of utilitarian women's panties and bras. The next drawer held women's socks.

Tom raised an eyebrow. "That explains the romance novel."

"Ben said Ebenezer lived in his mother's house up the hill. Did you see any other roads?"

"No. This was the only one and it's a dead end at this place."

"Bizarre. I guess we go back and tell Peter what we found."

35

On balmy summer days, it wasn't uncommon for the front door of the Rustler's Roost to be blocked open, letting fresh air and a sliver of sunlight into the usually dim interior. Mary, finished with business, typically spent her days on the stool farthest away from the door, preferring anonymity. This day, she sat on the closest stool, eye on Main Street. Earlier, she watched as Peter, Angus, and Tom left the sheriff's office in search of Ebenezer Hatcher. Several hours passed before she saw Peter drive by on his way to the courthouse. Sometime after that, she watched as Angus and then Tom drove past. Because of tinted windows in the police vehicles, she couldn't tell if any of them carried a prisoner. She also couldn't bring herself to wait for a call.

Mary signaled to Eddie. He poured a double shot of whiskey into an old-fashioned glass and slid it across the bar, then watched her light a cigarette with shaky hands.

"A double shot of the good stuff. Whatever's going on, it must be a dilly."

Mary tipped the glass back and emptied it in one swallow. She stubbed out her unfinished cigarette.

"I've got to go out for a while." She grabbed her purse and slipped it over her shoulder.

Eddie watched her go. Mary was rock solid. Whatever had her so shook wasn't good.

TRAVIS LOOKED OVER his shoulder as he stood in the doorway to Peter's office. Ben was eating a Brewery burger and fries with pure pleasure. Zack sat watching, more interested in Ben than the burger.

"I don't think he's had a burger and fries for a while. Good idea picking that up for him," said Peter.

"Do we know if this is the Ben who Stacey was talking about?"

"Unofficially. I sent a picture over to Jarod Nichols at the hospital. He showed it to Stacey, and she confirmed. Weird though, she was worried about what was going to happen to him."

"Stockholm syndrome?"

"Could be. She was talking about how sweet he was and how he reminded her of her grandpa. In the same breath, she admitted he abused her and kicked her into the mine shaft."

"So, what are we going to do?"

"We wait until he's full and happy and see if we can get any more information out of him. At this point he's at least complicit in Stacey's kidnapping. The doctor says she's still too weak to question."

They heard footsteps in the hallway and Tom and then Angus came into Peter's office.

"No Ebenezer?" asked Peter.

"No nobody," said Tom. "We found a house, but the whole thing was weird."

Tom and Angus took turns telling about the seemingly abandoned house with evidence of recent activity.

"A romance novel on the end table and women's clothes in the dresser," said Angus.

"YOU!!!!" The men heard a woman's voice yell in the outer office.

Travis, Angus, and Tom ran to the front office with Peter close behind them.

"YOU!!!" Mary yelled again as she hurled herself at Ben, knocking him off his folding chair. "You killed all those girls. You killed Faith." Mary broke down in tears as she pummeled Ben with her fists.

As Angus and Tom pulled Mary off Ben, he got to his feet, roaring in anger. Gone was the meek and open face of Ben. The man who stood in his place wore a mask of pure evil.

"That's Ebenezer!" said Mary.

Ebenezer balled his fist and swung hard at Mary's face. Peter caught the fist before it could make contact and twisted the arm downward. Ebenezer pulled free with strength brought on by murderous rage, launching himself toward Mary. Angus put his head down and propelled himself into the middle of the enraged man, knocking him to the ground. Tom swung Mary around to Travis, who picked her up by the waist and carried her into Peter's office. Angus and Ebenezer rolled across the floor.

"Take him, Zack," yelled Peter.

Zack latched onto the seat of Ebenezer's pants and Ebenezer let out a howl of pain.

Travis shut and locked the office door and sat Mary carefully on the leather couch. He dropped down next to her, shaking nearly as hard as Mary.

"I don't do drama well," he said.

"That was intense," said Mary, tears replaced by hysterical laughter.

In the outer office, Peter and Angus rolled the prisoner to his side and Tom snapped on a pair of handcuffs.

"Release, Zack," said Peter.

They lifted and dragged Ebenezer into a jail cell. Peter, Tom, and Angus hurried out and shut the door. They took deep breaths of relief while the prisoner threw himself around the cell in an insane frenzy.

"He's going to hurt himself," gasped Tom.

"Call Dr. Hamm. Tell him to bring a sedative."

Peter turned the knob on his office door, found it locked, and knocked.

"You can open the door now, Travis. We have Ben, or Ebenezer, or whoever he is cuffed and in the cell."

Travis unlocked and opened the door.

"Everyone okay in here?" asked Peter.

"Yeah, we're good," said Travis.

"Sorry about that, Peter," said Mary. "I guess I could have been a little more subtle."

"No argument there. What were you thinking?"

"I was thinking about Faith and all the other girls who've gone missing... and then I had a couple drinks." She pushed herself to her feet.

"Stay here, Mary. We don't want to antagonize him."

She sank back into the couch.

Peter picked up his phone and dialed the Missoula County Sheriff's office.

"Nick Patterson here."

"Answering your phone yourself these days, Nick?"

"Hey, Peter. Long time no hear. How're you doin'?"

"Crazy over here today. We have a prisoner who's more than a little nuts as far as I can tell. We called the local doctor to come over and administer a sedative."

"And you want me to take him off your hands?" guessed Nick.

"Sure would appreciate it. We don't have the personnel or jail space to keep him here."

"What do you have him on?"

"Kidnapping. Attempted murder. He may be a serial."

"Yikes. Okay, I'll make arrangements to receive. Let me know when you have transport worked out."

"Thanks, Nick. I appreciate you."

Peter put down the phone. The banging in the cell quieted, but the prisoner continued to rant incoherently. Dr. Hamm poked his head through the door.

"Hey, Doc. Thanks for coming over so fast."

"No problem, Peter. Office hours are done for the day. I'm going to need some help holding this guy down while I give him a B-52."

Peter hesitated, "I'm pretty sure you're not going to give him a bomber."

Doc laughed, "A B-52 is Haldol and Ativan. It'll calm that guy right down."

"How fast will it work and how long will it last?"

"He'll be down in fifteen minutes and out for twenty-four hours."

"Excellent! Let's do it."

Doc readied his shot while Peter lifted keys to the cell off a hook inside his door and called to Tom and Angus.

"We need to hold him still for a few seconds, long enough for Doc to get the shot in his arm."

"Got it," said both Tom and Angus.

The men were surprised to find Ebenezer sitting, face to the wall, muttering to himself. No reaction when Peter turned the key in the lock.

"Maybe he wore himself out," said Angus.

The door opened and Ebenezer stood, twirled, and launched himself toward the door faster than anyone would have thought possible.

Peter grabbed him around the waist. Angus and Tom each took a leg and flipped him onto the cell cot. Doc jabbed the readied syringe through Ebenezer's shirt sleeve and into the muscle of his arm.

He pulled out the needle and yelled, "GO!"

The four men stumbled and tripped over each other running to the cell door. They managed to get through the door and slam it shut before Ebenezer could roll himself off the cot. They were rewarded with high-pitched shrieks and feet kicking the bars to the cell. Relief came quickly as the drug took effect.

"I guess that solves the mystery of Ebenezer," said Angus.

"Who wants to transport him to Missoula?" asked Peter.

"Flip a coin?" asked Tom.

"No. You need to send him in an ambulance," said Doc. "We need to monitor his vital signs, breathing, and make sure he doesn't aspirate."

"Okay. Sure," said Peter.

He pulled out his cell phone and punched in the number for EMT Scott Haugen.

"Hey, Scott. Can you do a transport to Missoula?... yeah, we're assuming he's the kidnapper. He's sedated and Doc says he should be out for twenty-four hours. Tom will ride with you. Park in back, I don't want Mavis and the mayor to get wind of this."

Peter disconnected. "We're set. He's on his way."

He opened his office door.

"You can come out now, Mary. He's past being upset."

Mary happily left Peter's office.

"I need a drink," she said as she hurried out the door and down the hallway.

Scott and a paramedic loaded the snoring Ebenezer onto a stretcher and carried him down the back staircase. Tom followed them out.

"I'm still wondering," mused Angus, after they left. "Did he have an accomplice?"

"You're thinking about the women's clothes and romance novel?" asked Peter.

"Yeah."

"It's a mystery."

"Ben. Ebenezer. I don't know what to call him now."

"A rose by any other name…"

"It's weird," said Angus. "He's like two different people. When we met Ben, it's like Stacey said, he reminds me of everybody's favorite grandpa. When Mary called him Ebenezer he turned into a monster."

"I'm no psychologist, but maybe this is one of those multiple personality things."

"Have you ever seen a case like this before?"

"Can't say as I have. It's the Wild West out here, Angus. You never know what's going to walk in the door."

36

Peter sat at his desk, his long and lean frame enjoying the plush leather office chair delivered that afternoon from an anonymous donor. The plain white card simply stated 'Thank you' in ornate silver script. No signature. Thank you for what, Peter didn't know, but he'd take it. The chair tag called the color 'Burnished Bourbon' and claimed the leather would get softer with use. *Was that possible?* thought Peter, running his hands across the smooth leather as he tried out the swivel and tilt features of the chair.

"Wow, Boss," said Travis, watching from the doorway. "That chair classes up the place. No idea where it came from?"

"No idea," said Peter, thinking he should get 'no idea' tattooed on his forehead and save himself answering... or maybe on a T-shirt.

"Can I have your old chair?"

Peter laughed, "Sure. Run out of duct tape?"

Travis's chair was more duct tape than original material. Office equipment for the sheriff's office wasn't a priority in Stone County. "Shouldn't you be out catching criminals?" was the mayor's comment whenever Peter submitted a request. Peter, eyeing the top-of-the-line equipment in the mayor's office, wanted to ask, "Shouldn't you be out shaking hands and kissing babies?" But he didn't.

Travis moved the rolling display of duct tape from behind his desk. "What do you want me to do with this old chair?" he asked.

"Trash, unless you think you can get something for recycled duct tape. If they pay by weight, we could all go on vacation."

"Trash it is," laughed Travis.

Tired and cranky from a busy night shift, Helen straggled through the door.

"How did you get a new chair?" she asked Travis.

"Peter's old one. You should see his new one."

Helen followed Travis into Peter's office, where he demonstrated the swivel and tilt features. "Come feel this leather," he said.

Helen groaned with pleasure as she caressed the chair. "Does the mayor know how much this cost?" she asked.

Peter handed her the card. "Anonymous donor."

"Wow! No idea who it came from?"

"No idea."

"Can I have Travis's old chair?"

"The duct tape dream?"

"All I have is a metal folding chair." She glanced self-consciously at the uniform buttons straining around her expanding waist. "It's too small."

"That's it," said Peter, standing and moving around his desk. Three strides took him to the outer office and the ugly duct-taped chair. He heaved it to his shoulder and headed out the door.

Helen and Travis looked at each other in surprise. "Hey, where are you going with my chair?" called Helen.

"The mayor's office," yelled Peter, as he walked down the hallway to the stairs.

Mayor Kalinski became mayor only because the previous mayor, and more popular candidate, died of a heart attack on election night. The deceased incumbent won the race, but Dwight Kalinski was appointed by default. Mayor Kalinski led with greed, arrogance, and a 'me first' leadership philosophy. After his sham of an election, he rearranged the first floor of the courthouse to give himself a rather large corner office, forcing the four county clerks who previously occupied the room to cram into the much smaller suite historically used as the mayor's office.

Peter walked into Kalinski's office without knocking and past the desk of his anxious secretary.

"Peter," she called after him. "Peter. The mayor isn't in." She lurched out of her chair and tottered after him in stiletto heels.

Peter pulled the mayor's lush leather chair away from his desk and dropped the duct-taped junker in its place.

"What are you doing?" exclaimed the secretary.

"I don't mean to get you in trouble, Debbie, but when his highness returns, tell him if he thinks that piece of garbage is suitable for a county employee, he can come and get his chair back."

Debbie smiled gleefully. "He won't have the nerve."

She reached down and pulled off one shoe and then the other. "And I don't care what he says, the city dress code doesn't say I have to wear three-inch heels and a mini skirt."

With new-found courage, she dropped the heels into the mayor's trash can.

Peter grinned. "I think we have an extra pair of uniform pants in your size upstairs if you want to ditch that skirt."

"You're on!"

She helped Peter lug the chair upstairs and maneuver it through the door of the sheriff's office. "Here's your new chair, Helen," Peter said, as they set it down in front of Travis's desk.

Helen stood with her mouth open looking from Peter to Debbie and back to Peter.

"Really? For me?"

"Sure. Try it out."

Helen lowered herself into the chair, caressing the soft leather. Burgundy-dyed with a tufted seat back, it exuded elegance. "I may never go home," she said.

"Compliments of the mayor. Just don't mention it to him," said Peter, winking at Debbie. "Travis, do we have a pair of uniform pants that'll fit Debbie?"

"Sure, Boss," said Travis, looking nervously at Debbie, not wanting to guess her size.

"Size six should work," she said.

Relieved, Travis made his way to the storage closet, rifled through a pile of clothes and pulled out a pair of pants. "Here you go."

"You can change in the bathroom," said Peter, pointing her toward the far end of the room.

"Thanks, Peter."

Travis and Helen looked at Peter with raised eyebrows.

"New dress code in the mayor's office," he said.

LATER, THE CREW was gathered for an update on the abduction case.

"So, Ben, A.K.A. Ebenezer, admitted to kidnapping all those girls?" asked Birdie.

"As much of a confession as you can expect from an insane person," said Peter. "We have plenty of evidence without the confession. Stacey identified him as the man who held her captive, abused her, and kicked her into the cave, although the drugs he gave her blocked any memory of what happened between the brewery and his cabin. Tire casts taken at the cave-in site match Ben's truck. His and Stacey's fingerprints are all over Ben's cabin and Ben's fingerprints are at the house up the hill and on the business card. We can only speculate that she was lured in by the business card and got in the truck with him thinking she was going to a bed and breakfast."

"What about the women's clothes and the romance novel?" asked Angus.

"The clothes were his mother's. After she died, he left the house pretty much as it was and only went there when he was in his Ebenezer persona."

"And the romance novel?"

Peter laughed. "No, that was his. The local librarian said he reads them faster than she can get them in."

"How are you doing on cataloging those bones, Helen?" asked Tom.

"It's going to take a while. He's been doing this for a few decades."

"Is there any chance of identifying any of them?" asked Birdie.

"After we have them out of the cave, we'll send them to the state forensics lab. If we're lucky, some will ping DNA matches sent into those ancestry sites. The state also has a new forensics artist who specializes in facial reconstruction of skulls. Reconstructed faces have been recognized in the past. There's always a chance."

Birdie fingered the crystal necklace she wore around her neck. Selina's bones may never be officially identified, but she knew the truth.

Peter felt a darkness settling around his crew.

"Let's go to the grill for ribs," he said.

The mood brightened as fast it had dimmed, everyone racing to the door.

All kids at heart, thought Peter, smiling to himself.

The crew filled the largest table at the grill, Tom saving a seat for his wife who was on her way.

Peter was surprised to see the mayor's secretary, Debbie Tonapah, handing out menus.

"Moonlighting, Debbie?" asked Peter.

"No. New job. His highness the mayor had issues with my new dress code. He wrote me up for insubordination over the whole chair incident, but I know it was because I refused to wear stilettos and a mini skirt."

"Gosh, I'm sorry, Debbie. That whole chair thing was my doing."

"I should thank you. You got me away from that creep."

"I can do one better. Things are hopping at the sheriff's office. We could use extra help in the clerk/dispatch department. It would free Travis to help with forensics. Come over to the office tomorrow and pick up an application."

"Really?! Oh, wow. I mean, waitressing is a step up from working for the mayor but working in the sheriff's office would be even better."

She leaned over and whispered toward the crew at the table. "Don't mention it until I'm off shift or I won't get my share of the tips."

She got thumbs up around the table.

"Ribs for everyone?" Debbie asked, noticing the pile of unopened menus stacked in the middle of the table.

"Yep."

37

ARLY ONE JULY morning, oblivious to the beauty surrounding them, a somber group gathered on the mountain hillside above Stony Clairmont's rustic cabin. A large flat granite stone, taken from the surrounding mountains, covered what once was a caved-in mine shaft. The opening intentionally covered to ensure no other lives would be lost to that cave, and the stone a reminder of the many women callously tossed into darkness and death. Inset into the stone, a bronze plaque depicting a gruff seaman and his pup, the heroes who found and saved the life of the last victim. Names of the other victims were not available, and Stacey Nichols respectfully declined an invitation to have hers added. She wanted to never be reminded of her harrowing ordeal.

A keepsake box, formed of resin and stone and adorned with meadow flowers, stood at the side of the plaque. Mary stepped forward, opened the lid and gently placed a smooth river rock in the bottom of the box. Etched into the rock, the single word *Faith*. Birdie followed Mary. Her offering, a necklace of beads holding a deep brown colored crystal. Stony knelt and gave a small pink collar to Lizbeth who, following the lead of the women, dropped it into the box. Stony closed the lid, and the group bowed their heads as Paul Elliot said a prayer for the women who were lost and forgotten to all except that small group.

⋅•◦•⋅

RECLINING IN HIS easy chair, feet up and open Cold Smoke in his hand, Peter should have been a content man. A case solved and the victim alive and on the road to recovery was a feather in any lawman's hat. It was not lost on him, however, that the kidnapping and recovery of Stacey Nichols was ultimately solved by civilians, Stony Clairmont and Mary. Memories of Mavis and Mayor Kalinski and their accusations of his inadequacy troubled his mind. Had he missed clues through the years?

Abandoned cars towed with no investigation? He studied the file on his lap, his parents' murder file. When the time came, when he could bring himself to open the file, would he be up to the task? Could he solve his own parents' murder? Peter set the file back in its place next to his chair, sipped his beer, and washed away the memories, if only for a while.

Thank you for reading Innocence Slain!

Have you considered leaving a review? Reviews help me spread the word and help other readers decide if they want to enjoy the book, too.

Please scan the QR code below and let me know what you think! :)

-Kit

GET YOUR FREE EBOOK

Join the citizens of Anderson in *Mountain Tales,* an ever-growing collection of short stories about past and present mysteries.

SIGN UP AT KITKARSON.COM

BOOK 3 IS HERE

A much-despised newcomer to Anderson is found dead at the dump. Sheriff Elliott and his deputies investigate to find the killer and save themselves.

FIND IT AT KITKARSON.COM/BOOKS

www.ingramcontent.com/pod-product-compliance
Lightning Source LLC
Chambersburg PA
CBHW021217310726
48971CB00006B/1591